KANE COULD BARELY MAKE OUT THE SHAPES IN FRONT OF HIM.

IF HE HADN'T LIVED THROUGH THE PAST HOURS he might have thought . . . *dogs. There are three dogs in front of me. Cutting me off.*

But he could be sure that they weren't dogs. Even in the half-light he could see that they looked like the things he blew to pieces in the restroom above. He didn't ask himself what they were then . . . and he wasn't going to now.

One of the creatures moved to the side. He saw another look back as if considering moving in another direction. Which is when the third one leaped at him.

The creature's powerful hind legs sent it—so big and bulky—flying right at him. More of the animal came into the light and Kane could see the head. A gaping hole filled with teeth . . .

MAELSTROM

MATTHEW COSTELLO

BASED ON THE VIDEO GAME
DOOM 3 **FROM ID SOFTWARE**

Pocket Star Books
New York   London   Toronto   Sydney

Pocket Star Books
A Division of Simon & Schuster, Inc.
1230 Avenue of the Americas
New York, NY 10020

This book is a work of fiction. Names, characters, places, and incidents either are products of the author's imagination or are used fictitiously. Any resemblance to actual events or locales or persons, living or dead, is entirely coincidental.

First Pocket Star Books paperback edition April 2009

POCKET STAR and colophon are registered trademarks of Simon & Schuster, Inc.

For information about special discounts for bulk purchases, please contact Simon & Schuster Special Sales at 1-800-456-6798 or business@simonandschuster.com.

The Simon & Schuster Speakers Bureau can bring authors to your live event. For more information or to book an event contact the Simon & Schuster Speakers Bureau at 866-248-3049 or visit our website at www.simonspeakers.com.

Design by Alan Dingman
Art by Robert Hunt

Manufactured in the United States of America

10 9 8 7 6 5 4 3 2 1

ISBN-13: 978-1-4165-5385-4
ISBN-10:   1-4165-5385-1

To Tim Willits . . .
A good person to know on Earth . . . and Mars . . . when
the monsters come.

2145

TWO DAYS BEFORE
THE FIRST
OUTBREAK

1

DAVID RODRIGUEZ LOOKED AT A SEISMIC map of the ocean floor, focusing on the mammoth Mid-Atlantic Ridge—the world's greatest mountain chain, although miles under the surface of the ocean.

He saw a massive network of fissures—potential problem areas—all at different depths, spread throughout the ridge. Each area fed a steady stream of real-time information to the lab's computers.

Only days ago the lab got an early warning about a good-sized plate shift that was bound to produce some major fissures. But the information coming from the probes—detailing the stress to the continental plates, the depth of bedrock, the possible path of erupting magma—showed that the Ballard Lab itself was not in any danger. Good thing too. An evacuation would be costly, not to mention years of work lost down the hydrothermal tube.

But the probes also showed that this latest seismic spur would create a new series of thermal spouts not too far from the lab.

David turned back to the open work area behind him. Giant tanks housed specimens, all surrounded by teams of his scientists working at self-contained modules near the tanks. No closed offices or lab rooms here—as lab director, David Rodriguez had a say in the design and he wanted everyone coming down here to feel that no matter what they were working on, they were all part of a team.

What one discovers, we all discover, he always told them.

And though practically everyone down here was bristling with credentials—many more so than others—there would be no "Doctor this" or "Doctor that." Including Rodriguez himself.

"¿Ola, Tomas, cómo van las cosas hoy?"

Tomas, who held advanced degrees in genetic microbiology and molecular physics, looked up and smiled. *"Muy bien,* David. Though we hope to get our hands on some of the new samples"—he nodded his head to the great ocean past the massive walls of the lab—"out there."

David laughed. "I'm going out there soon. Just waiting until things settle down a bit." He turned to the big 3-D view of the ocean floor behind him. "So far, things are looking good."

"I know. This really could be the opportunity we've been waiting for."

David nodded in agreement, and started for the east end of the podlike lab.

Amazingly, the design of the lab's transport pod was based on an old vid about space travel. Even the submersibles were modeled on the shape of the EVA vehicles on the spaceship in that film called *2001*, now nearly 200 years old. Not that anyone really watched the old vids anymore.

But that carefully researched design for space made absolutely perfect sense for the deep ocean environment, where the pressure could get close to one thousand atmospheres and the temperature plunged to well below the zero mark, though nothing ever froze thanks to the water salinity.

The door to the submersible bay opened, and Julie Chao walked in.

"Morning," David said quickly.

Once they had been together, back at Woods Hole—partners in life and in science. Not anymore. But when he planned the lab, he knew he'd want Julie working with the team. Both thought they could get past their past. Easier said than done, David realized.

But then, they both worked hard to remain professional and to avoid any letting down of their guard and slipping into—what? Friendship?

Remembrance? Nostalgia for the good times they had? Or maybe bitterness at how and why it ended?

"Is it morning? I gave up keeping track of when it's day or night. How quaint of you to keep it up," Julie remarked.

He smiled. She always did have a bit of an edge.

"Right. Okay, everything all checked out at your end?"

Julie nodded, even as she slipped into the bulky suit that would provide an extra measure of temperature protection should they hit an area where the thermal currents spiked and the water went from below zero to two hundred degrees in seconds.

"Yup, all set. Everyone's excited about getting samples from the new vents."

"I know. Completely virgin compounds in the process of being—I don't know—born."

She laughed at that. "If you can call it birth." Then she looked at him. "You *are* coming along with me, right?"

David nodded. "Right. I'll suit up. We'll take submersible number one."

"Doesn't matter to me."

With that, David started getting into his suit, checking as he did that the biometric functions kicked in, tracking all his vital signs, sending the information to the lab. When he was ready, the technicians opened up the first sub door and David followed Julie into the incredibly tight space.

"Okay. All set here," David said.

"Roger, David. Airlock closed behind you. Julie, all your equipment reading okay?"

"Everything's fine," Julie said.

"Right. Ejection in thirty seconds."

They sat there and waited. David turned to Julie, who looked straight ahead, eyes on the Christmas tree—like an array of colorful buttons and lights. The submersible had three small ports, one dead ahead and two others to the side. Because of the tremendous pressure, the windows to the outside world had to be small, and the reinforced polymer "glass" inches thick.

The sub was silently and smoothly ejected through the airlock.

The outside cameras provided a much better view than could be seen in the port in front of either passenger. Now the screens above them showed the view as the sub glided away from the lab toward the underwater mountain range, the Mid-Atlantic Ridge.

Years ago, David's team had navigated and mapped a series of valleys that cut into the nearest undersea mountains. David knew which valley gave them a clear shot to HTVR-1138—the new Hydrothermal Vent Region 1138.

Now Julie guided the sub between two massive mounds with just enough space to slip between them. Some abyssal creatures, a light-dangling angler fish and the always bizarre pelican gulper eel, came by to explore.

They don't get many visitors around here.

"Everything good, Julie?"

"Yup—nice and smooth. The temp readings are about what we'd expect."

David knew that these subs were not the newest toys out of the UAC's box. Their real attention stayed locked on Mars and the much-vaunted Mars City. This deep-ocean lab had turned into a neglected sideshow for Kelliher and his team of advisers in California.

Was the day coming that it would be shut down? That could well happen if nothing practical came out of the lab, and soon. The lab had been promoted to the world as a general oceanic research center specializing in finding new methods of desalinization and use of ocean resources, but David knew that— for the UAC—there was a much larger goal. Toward which there had been very little progress.

"Whoa—there's something!" Julie tapped a button in front of her.

David looked down and saw that the outside water temperature was beginning to spike. Which meant that a current of superheated water had just hit the sub.

"Think we're okay to go on?"

"For now. But we best watch it. Got the new vent field coming up dead ahead."

David looked at the large screen above their heads. Twin Cameron lenses provided a wavy 3-D image of the world ahead—wavy due to the blurring effect of the volcanically heated water.

And as the sub glided forward almost soundlessly, both of them gazed at a sight that simply never became anything less than staggering.

First they saw the crab colonies—gatherings of giant albino crabs that, unlike their more prosaic seashore cousins, worked and hunted together, acting more like ants. The fact that they were bleach-white and each was the size of a kitchen table always made the initial glimpse of this alternate world an amazing one.

Then they spotted other crustaceans hanging around the periphery, perhaps hoping to scarf up whatever the crabs left over. One of them—for David, the most disturbing creature down here—was the gyanthomous, an isopod the size of a golden retriever. To witness it was to think that it was impossible that it came from Earth.

"Tube worms coming up," Julie said.

From out of the mist of blurry volcanic water and flecks of debris, David watched the field of tube worms appear. These worms—some standing twenty to thirty feet tall—were the true dominant life-form down here. The tube worms hosted the parasitic bacteria that somehow took the sulfurous water, poisonous to any other creature, and turned it into food that the worms then consumed. A perfect and incredible symbiotic relationship. And the fact that the food produced resembled hemoglobin in its chemical makeup was still something that confused scientists, even a hundred years after the worms' discovery by Robert Ballard. Many of the station's best teams worked on finding out where this life came from, how it developed, and how it might evolve in the future.

Julie edged the small sub up and sailed it above the massive tube worm field, as the worms repeatedly sucked in the poisonous water, each feeding its own colony of bacteria. The sharp temperature spike—the stray current—seemed to have veered away.

"Always something to see, isn't it?" David said.

"That's for sure."

Something—as in a complete ecosystem that has absolutely nothing to do with photosynthesis. Nothing to do with any system of life found on the surface at all. This was as close to an alien world as David could imagine.

Yet, here it was, ancient, thriving—and David, along with the others on his team, felt it had things to say. About planet Earth. About humanity. Maybe about humanity's ability to survive.

Let everyone else keep their eyes on Mars. For David, down here was where the real mystery of life lay.

"Okay, going to start heading over toward the new vents," Julie said.

David nodded as she banked the submersible to the right, away from this mature vent field, away from the looming "smokers" ahead—the mini-volcano-like openings—to where Mother Earth had just recently cracked open a bit more.

And life—a different kind of life—was about to begin.

2

"THERE WE ARE," JULIE SAID, LEANING CLOSER to the porthole.

"Got a better view on the screen here."

She turned to David and smiled. "I like seeing the *real* thing. I'm kinda old-school that way." Julie turned back to the screen.

David looked at the 3-D image, which made it appear as if the open fissures and new smokers were inside the submersible.

"Always amazing," he said. "The earth opens up, and hundreds of degrees of molten magma gets squeezed out. Beautiful—"

"Yeah, and a bit terrifying, too. We best get busy gathering the samples."

David leaned down and grabbed the handle-like grip of the controllers for the sub's left arm. The controllers allowed for a variety of deep-ocean operations. To start, David began collecting water samples, the amount of sulfurous and chemical material rising with each sample. Julie did the same thing with the other arm, but then she stopped and took the submersible down a few feet closer to the surface.

"Now for some bottom grabs," she announced. The goal was to get a range of samples that showed the increased concentration of the strange chemical mixture, which might lead to an understanding of the origins of this bizarre ecosystem of hydrothermal vents.

David hit some control buttons for his exterior arm, and now the claw shifted and he could carefully scoop the top layer of ocean bottom material, which already bore a frosting of the debris that drifted over from the smokers.

"How you doing?" Julie asked.

"Good. And the temps? Time to turn around?"

"Whoa—yeah. Must be a big fissure. Heat's getting up there fast. We got what everyone wanted. New material, freshly deposited. So—"

David looked up at the screen. The open fissure was closer now, the new chimneylike smokers pouring out a steady stream of superheated water and magma. He waited, expecting to see the submersible start rising and then sharply banking away for the volcanic area ahead. When it didn't move, he said, "Julie?"

"We've got a problem. . . . Engine's not responding. We're heading straight toward the new vent area."

"Umm . . . ideas?"

"I—"

David could see the other controls responding

normally, including the temperature gauges, which
now began to sound a single shrill beep. Not loud,
not yet—

"Julie? It's your call."

She turned to him. "Really? Okay, I'm thinking."
She shook her head. Whatever it was she was going
to do, it better be damn fast. "Okay. My call. Only
one thing I can see that we can do. Shut the whole
thing down. Then a full system restart and hope the
engine controls come back online."

"What . . . are we in the Stone Age? Turn it off?"

"You said it's my call. It's all—"

"Fine. Do it."

As fast as she could, Julie hit the master control
switches that shut down every system on the submersible, from the air scrubbers to the massive inter-
connected electronics packed into the small sub.

Then . . . they floated, suspended in the dark, still
only feet from the bottom, the air immediately turning stale, the temperature climbing by the second.

David held his breath, knowing that Julie would
wait a precious few more seconds until she thought
every system was truly down and off. He tried not to
count.

Then he heard her: "Okay." She started to throw
the switches, moving faster than he ever saw any
human move before. She followed the standard progression, internal electronics, system monitoring,
outside data electronics, air scrubber, and finally
main and secondary thrusters.

The warning beep immediately returned, but now as a steady, constant ping that was deafening. David forced himself to look away from the temperature screens. He didn't need confirmation of what he could feel.

And once again they waited.

"Here goes," Julie said.

The scrubbers had returned to their job of providing clean air, but the air was so hot that David breathed only when he had to. Glowing streams of magma filled the porthole screens.

3

THE ALARM NEARLY DROWNED OUT THE whirring of the engines. But in a second, David saw the glowing smokers up close, ready to toast the sub, quickly vanish from the portholes as the sub finally arced upward. Then the sub made a sharp tilt to the right as Julie banked it, giving it all the juice she could.

There were no cheers, no exultations over a close call, because it was still anybody's guess as to whether they could clear the vent field with enough leeway to avoid frying the sub's systems. Because if that happened, they'd probably drop down to the field and bake.

All they did was sit silently and hope that the power of the engines and the angle of the bank would suffice. *Please*, David thought, *let it be enough.*

A few more moments, and the sub kept arcing away. But now David saw Julie level it off, keeping the engines at full throttle.

Then—a gift—the pinging stopped. The temperature still read dangerously high—a couple of hundred degrees outside—but now it started falling steadily.

David turned to Julie, feeling, as he often did, that persistent pull toward his ex. Sometimes breaking up with her seemed like the dumbest thing he had ever done. Or did she break up with him? Even *that* they could not agree on.

"You did good."

"Could have gone either way," she answered. Only then a small smile. "Like I said, I'm old-school. When in doubt, reboot."

"Or kick the tires."

A small laugh from both of them now that the threat of what would have been a quick and intense death had passed.

"Let's go home," he said.

"You got it," Julie said.

And they sat amid the colorful lights, the air finally beginning to cool, both glad to be alive.

When they arrived back at the lab, David slipped out of his suit, clammy from the heat and humidity that, no matter what the scrubbers did, always somehow filled the submersible.

A crew worked at the front of the small sub, removing the pressurized sample cases. The material was good only as long as the temperature and pressure remained constant.

Julie said a few words to the lab crew, and then came over to David.

"I'm going to follow these inside. In case there are any questions."

"And there will be. I'll make sure engineering starts taking the sub apart to see what the hell went wrong."

Julie turned and looked at the vehicle that nearly cost them their lives. "Age, probably. What is it? Tech from ten years ago?"

"Maybe earlier. This lab has stopped being a UAC priority."

She laughed at that. "It would be one if it was on Mars."

"Or Europa."

She looked at him when he said that. David knew from their discussions that there were many things about this project that no one, not even the various scientific teams working on it, were aware of. But he and Julie also knew that it had a number of hidden goals way beyond economical desalinization and deep-ocean aquaculture.

And one of those goals was squarely centered on the frozen moon of Europa.

Frozen, that is, until you penetrated a few thousand feet of ice to the open sea below. Where, as any planetary geologist or biologist could tell you, anything might await.

"Okay, then. You go with the samples. I'll catch up with you later."

He watched Julie return to the team while he waited for the engineering head to arrive.

Chief Engineer Ozzie Stern, a thin, wiry man who, as far as David could remember, never smiled, listened while David described the sub's failure.

Then Ozzie took a deep breath. "I keep telling you, David. These subs, I mean, jeez . . ." He shook his head. "How can you expect to keep them running? They're all *way* beyond a full overhaul. If you want my opinion—"

David smiled. "Not sure that I do. . . ."

No smile came back from Ozzie. "They should all be junked. Every damn one of them. Maybe used for parts. Put in some damn museum."

"Good. Glad you got that off your chest. But what can you do for now"—David put a hand on Ozzie's shoulder—"is to make sure that what just happened doesn't happen again."

"I don't know. I'll look. We'll do our best. But no promises."

"Got it. That's all I can ask."

David started to head toward the Bio Pod, but a few steps away he stopped and turned. "Oh, and if you can have them ready by, say, tomorrow, that would be just great."

Ozzie shook his head like some disapproving father.

But as David walked away, he knew that the sub's problem—at least the engine issues—would be solved by then. Ozzie was moody as hell, but he never disappointed.

The Biolab, the most secure area of the Ballard research station, could only be accessed by a select few teams at the station. Everything that went on here was, for lack of a better description, top secret.

David put his palm up for a scan, then entered his password. It all seemed a bit excessive.

As he walked in, he could see the teams already working feverishly. A trio of screens showed the bacteria-filled water magnified to the point where the samples looked like distant star systems.

Only here the "planets" whizzed madly around each other, pulsating.

Except this wasn't really life. What was happening here, what was happening in the whole ecosystem of the hydrothermal vents, was really something else. You could almost call it anti-life. Organisms that could make food out of poisonous chemicals, and then provide that food to other organisms.

The bacteria took the poisonous sulfurous water and *thrived* on it, turning it into food that nourished the giant tube worms and ultimately fed everything that lived in the superheated world of the vents.

So many questions remained. Which was why Ian Kelliher of the UAC funded this station: he wanted answers. But apparently he also wanted more than that from *this* work.

"How are the samples looking?" asked David, standing behind Julie.

She bent over a microscope, choosing to examine the bacteria colony in the traditional way rather than with the 3-D screens.

"Great. The best we've had. I mean"—she straightened up and turned to David—"we've had good samples before, but they were always further along in the process." She pointed to one of the screens. "See that cluster there? Never really caught that before. The bacteria coming together and making a small colony. As if exchanging information before they— Hey! There, look."

David watched a cluster explode apart.

"They do that over and over. It has to serve some purpose before they begin producing the by-product that feeds the worms."

"Almost like—" David caught himself. The idea was too outlandish.

But Julie prodded him. "What? What were you going to say?"

"Almost as if they were exchanging DNA information. Like strands of the helix coming together, matching up. Crazy idea."

But Julie shook her head. "No, not so crazy. I mean, what else can we compare it to?"

David looked up at the computer monitors above each of the screens. "A lot of data coming in."

"Yes. It'll take weeks to analyze it all. Then we can let these bacteria begin their life cycle, and track that. But—for the first time—we will have monitored them from the very beginning."

"Great. I'll go give the boss a report. He'll be pleased."

"Maybe tell him about the subs? Drop a hint we could use some new ones."

"Oh, yeah. He'd *love* to hear that. I think I'll tell him right after he mentions he's pulling the plug on this whole project."

"Maybe just one new sub?"

Sharif Aziz, one of Julie's team, looked up. "And maybe a few more bacteriologists. I'd like to get some sleep one of these days."

"Sleep?" David said. "What's that?"

They laughed. *A good sound,* David thought as he turned away and headed to his office, where a report to Ian Kelliher—head of the United Aerospace Corporation—had to be filed. Hooray, the fun part of the day was over.

4

THE SCREENS ON DAVID'S DESK SHOWED various newsfeeds covering the wonderful state of the surface world.

Every day seemed pretty much the same: always a scattering of skirmishes and near wars across the globe as people fought over the planet's dwindling resources. Politicians made promises, or threats, sometimes both simultaneously. Some corners of the Earth now seemed to be in constant turmoil as factions tried to assert their power over each other.

Then, there was Mars. A world away. "The Bright Red Hope," as described in UAC promotional material. David had to wonder: Did people really buy into that? That somehow the Red Planet, so far away, could offer hope to this world?

The UAC didn't, on the other hand, talk much about the Ballard sea lab. After all, while great strides have been made toward desalinization, making clean water more affordable and more readily available, the process still remained, for most of the planet, prohibitively expensive.

Such a simple matter, removing salt from water. It would be interesting if such an easy solution played a key role in the death of the late, great planet Earth. The water planet . . . and everyone on it dying of thirst.

But you could search all of the UAC's official literature and find nothing about the work going on in the undersea lab. Only Kelliher and handpicked members of his board received David's classified reports. And though David didn't care much for Kelliher or his methods, he did believe in what they were trying to do here. If they showed some success, it could lead to saving life on Earth.

And were they close? Hard to tell. Breakthroughs seemed to loom around each corner—amazing discoveries, incredible possibilities. But he knew that Kelliher wanted—no, *demanded*—more than simply discoveries and possibilities. He wanted concrete results that the biological processes the lab explored down here could actually work.

David rubbed his eyes. After the last trip to the new vent site, he felt fatigued, tired from the stress, the exertion—or maybe simply exhausted by all the responsibility.

But Kelliher wanted his damned report right away. Well, at least it would only be a one-sided conversation.

David flipped a switch that activated the camera above the central screen above him. He hit some keys, switching from the live newsfeed to a screen on which he could access the entire lab's database.

He entered his password, then opened up the directory, named by Ozzie Stein, whose Munich roots were showing. *Wurm.*

"Evening, Ian. I hope this report finds you in good spirits. I see, by the way, that work on Mars is moving right along." David smiled at the camera. "Someday you'll have to arrange a visit for me. Down here, we're also keeping busy. And some interesting things have been happening. But first—"

David touched the floating keypad, and an image box appeared in the corner of the screen. "The subs are giving us a problem. I know you said that there was nothing you could do now. I know—funding's tight. But, well, you see . . . Julie and I were nearly killed this morning thanks to a malfunction in one of the subs. Ozzie is looking all the subs over, but it's simply a matter of age. If you could—I don't know—but if we could get just *one* sub built to our specifications, well, it might save a life in the near future."

Always the sales pitch. Like a beggar asking for a handout. How many times had David done this, and how many times had Kelliher counseled patience?

"If you could, Ian, just see what you can do. We're very close down here, very close. So a new state-of-the-art submersible could make a big difference."

And that was all true enough, David thought.

"Okay, now to the good news. We've successfully recovered early samples of the *Dermatasporangium* bacteria, at what looks like a primary stage of what

Julie calls their 'grouping' process. We captured it all, and it will tell us a lot more about how they begin producing food and supporting the tube worm colony. But that's not all—"

David touched some more of the holographic keys floating to his side.

"Our experiments on creating an artificial skin modeled on the tube worm's exterior covering continues to be successful. The hemoglobin content, which you know is high in the worms, is still far removed from human hemoglobin. But we think, if we can track the progress of the bacteria, we can see where it diverges from human hemoglobin."

David took a breath. He wasn't sure he was going to tell Kelliher the next bit. But maybe, just maybe, it might allow some more funding to flow.

"I've sent you the experiment vids. If you get a chance—I know you're busy with Mars—but take a look. We think we've made a bit of a breakthrough, and by using the bacteria to regulate the artificial worm skin's development, we think we will soon have a key piece of the puzzle. We might actually be able to create a new form of synthetic skin that can self-replicate, along with a way to create virtually limitless human hemoglobin."

David watched the image and vid files upload, and in a second they were on the UAC's Palo Alto system, also securely locked.

"We're close. So close. And as you know, if we crack this, well, you understand the next prize."

The next prize. There was one that David had never believed in. But now? It all looked possible.

"Okay, Ian. Call, if you like, when you digest all of this." Knowing that Kelliher rarely called. Things were much too busy in the UAC for the company head to actually call the deep-ocean station. "That's it for now."

David gave the camera one last smile, and then, with a wave of his hand, the news returned.

As David lay in bed, almost sleeping, he heard a knock on his small cabin door.

"Yeah? Come in."

Julie opened the door a crack. "Oh, sorry. Thought, well, you'd still be up."

"That's okay. What's up?" David immediately noticed that Julie's face seemed tense, her eyes narrowed. She also had to be exhausted, because she tended to linger at the lab stations. Especially after what they'd brought in today. . . .

"It's something that just happened. *Is happening*, really. One of Sharif's team. It's something we both approved, no biggee."

"You look—I don't know—confused."

A bit of a smile. "Yeah, you could say that. Want to get up? Come and look. Better than talking about it." She took a breath, and David had that feeling that something was about to occur that would change things.

Still dressed, he slid out of his bunk and followed Julie back to the lab pod.

•   •   •

Three other biologists stood around Sharif, who sat before a trio of tanks, all monitored with cameras recording everything.

David walked up to them. "What do we have?"

Sharif turned back to him, his eyes wide. What was it that had the normally placid Sharif excited?

"It's what we've done before, David. With the bacteria samples. But we never had them at this early a stage. So—"

"Hold on," Julie interrupted. "Start at the beginning, Sharif."

Sharif took a breath. "In there—we started as soon as you brought the samples back." He pointed to the three tanks, all with a variety of sea life swimming about, looking not much different from any aquarium's installation. "Every animal in the tank has a series of microtransmitters either embedded or attached to its body. In addition, the 3-D cameras catch all their movements and heat registers."

Julie turned to David. "Our standard SOP. We injected some of the creatures with bacteria, and in other specially regulated tanks, we simply introduced the bacteria into the environment."

"It didn't matter," Sharif said flatly. "Either way, it just . . . didn't matter." He hit some keys and the live feed from the tanks disappeared from the three screens, replaced by recorded images from twenty-eight minutes ago. "Look at the crab. He's one we injected. He just froze up. We thought we had killed him. Now—okay, this is weird. Watch this."

As David looked on, the crab seemed to raise its arms in a move that almost seemed to suggest a sudden surge of power. Then, with a breathtakingly fast movement, it somehow kicked itself off the bottom and latched onto a silvery blue fish nearly four times its size.

David watched the claws make short work of cutting into the fish, sending a spray of blood and guts into the water.

But the pieces of the fish didn't last long there. As if they'd been waiting, other creatures in the tank swooped in, sharklike in their speed and determination, until in seconds not a bit of the fish was left.

"Wow."

"Wow, indeed," said Julie.

David leaned closer to the screen. "Am I crazy, or did that crab change? The claws somehow—"

Sharif nodded. "They're bigger. Yes, they're bigger! In minutes."

David looked around at the other animals. "And the others in the tank—"

Sharif froze the images and tapped the screen directly in front of him. "Check out the baby barracuda. Normally hides behind that chunk of coral over there, trying to stay out of the other fishes' way. Not after we introduced the bacteria."

David watched as the small barracuda, missile-like, jetted right at a much bigger fish, drilling into it. Like the crab, it was all over in a matter of minutes.

"You have got to be kidding me. And for the animals not injected?"

Sharif actually grinned at that. "That's the most interesting thing. For some, it didn't matter whether they were injected or just came in contact with the bacteria in the water. They all reacted pretty much the same."

Sharif let the images begin rolling again, and it grew impossible to keep track of the animals as some moved swiftly to destroy the others until, at the end, only a handful remained.

"The survivors . . ." David said.

"Precisely."

He turned to Julie. "There are two things I don't get." He shook his head. "Maybe more, but, well, start with just the two."

"Go ahead."

"First, how come we haven't seen this before?"

"Sharif has a theory. . . ."

Sharif nodded. "Yes, all the other samples had already passed through whatever phase this was. There must be a window where this . . . *event* . . . can happen. We've never seen it before because we always got the samples much too late."

"And your other question?" Julie asked.

"I thought—*we* thought—that the bacteria had a symbiotic relationship with the tube worms. Hell, with the entire hydrothermal vent community. This . . . doesn't look too symbiotic."

"Right. So that must mean—" Sharif paused.

David could fill in the blank. "It may not be a symbiotic relationship at all?"

No one said anything for a moment. The whole thrust of the work in these labs was to explore the ecosystem and bio-modifications of the vent life to see how it might be adapted for human use—might even save humanity from disappearing from the planet. But if the entire foundation, the whole premise, of the experiments was wrong, what then?

"I also have a question, not that any of us has an answer," Julie said, turning back to the live screen and the tanks, which now held only a fraction of the sea life they once contained. "And it's about the bacteria. What's happening now with them, inside these animals? Is it like some kind of infection, which has now passed, or—"

"Yeah. Or is it like the tube worms, and maybe not so symbiotic at all."

"Exactly."

David took a step closer, going right up to the glass, looking at the dull fish eyes as they looked back. "For now, let's hold off playing with these guys. I want us to check all the data, look at the vid records again, check everything. I don't want one of these animals taken out until we know for sure what happened."

A moment of silence. Then Julie said, "Or what may happen."

5

IAN KELLIHER SHUT OFF THE VID DISPLAY floating over his desk. He liked David Rodriguez, but truth be told, the clock was ticking on the expensive and, so far, not very useful undersea lab.

Still, it had all been worth a shot. That's why they called it research, after all. And Kelliher knew he had much bigger issues to deal with. In just thirty-six hours he would start getting some more important and credible reports from Mars, thanks to his sending Elliot Swann and Jack Campbell to Mars City. Both were totally loyal, and Campbell for one would let none of General Hayden's or Dr. Malcolm Betruger's bullshit get in his way.

Kelliher needed that information fast. The daily reports from his own labs, in the lower levels of the UAC campus, grew ever more confusing. *Disturbing.*

His attempt to monitor Betruger by having his team here explore similar avenues of research hadn't worked out too well.

Either Betruger was lying, or there was something specific about Mars that changed the experiments. Kelliher's dreams of teleportation seemed further away than ever.

Then of course there was the case of the Ballard lab. That once shining ray of hope that so far had produced little, if anything. And now David Rodriguez was looking for more money, a new sub, just when Kelliher was thinking that he should close the whole thing down. Not that the lab constituted a majority of UAC's financial resources—Mars City was UAC's financial sump pump, sucking as much out of the company as it could.

Ian's father would be mighty unhappy to see how low the company's capital had fallen. And what of the experiments themselves, the promise of new revolutionary technology for the company? Old Tommy Kelliher had always acted on instinct, a maverick in everything he did and touched. He was the one person that Ian could talk to and get some feedback that—despite Tommy's advanced age and a body held together by every medical breakthrough of the last half century—could still be sharp and incisive.

Kelliher pressed the side of the button-sized microphone on his jacket lapel. "Sharon, tell Sam I'm ready to go. And no escort, please. I don't want a lot of attention."

"Yes, Mr.—"

Ian touched the button again, cutting her off, and then he got his collection of images and charts together. Tommy Kelliher was old-school—if he looked at anything, he wanted to hold it in his hands, not see it floating before him like, as he put it, "some goddamn smoke in the goddamn wind."

Ian Kelliher hurried out of the office and down to the indoor car park.

A voice came from behind him. "Sir, I do wish that you'd allow—"

Ian nodded. Sam had been his driver for ten years, right out of the military, a decorated lieutenant who didn't mind this extravagantly well-paid job of chauffeur. Of course, that role was also amplified by the fact that Ian Kelliher required someone who was completely comfortable around weapons.

"Yeah, I know—you want me to have an escort. But then everyone knows my business, Sam. *Everyone* sees the boss heading out, chattering about where I might be going and why. Rumors, Sam—I don't need them."

"It's safety that I'm concerned about, sir."

"Yeah, well, they haven't invented the bullet that can penetrate the glass and body of this car."

Sam looked back, "There are bombs, sir, a well-placed thermo-charge as we drive over and—"

Ian laughed. "Just don't drive over any, okay?" Besides the armored body of the car, there was a small arsenal up front available to Sam. If anyone was foolish enough to try to stop the vehicle, they'd face some of the best counterterrorism training that the USA and UAC could provide.

Ian turned and looked back at the sleek, castle-like profile of the main UAC building. Only two stories or so above ground, the heart of the head-quarters, but a maze of labs lay unseen below, sur-rounded by a protective shell of bedrock.

The massive gate ahead opened, picking up the ID of the vehicle and actually scanning the passengers.

In minutes, they entered what was left of the California highway system. The interstate highways were hardly maintained at all anymore. Costs ren-dered that impossible, and troubles with a basic fuel supply meant that fewer people actually had need of them. Most of the other vehicles on the road here either had access to a private fuel supply, or—like Ian's own car—sported what was essentially an earthbound version of the ion engine. Unbelievably expensive, rendering it really useless for ordinary travel, the engine required no fossil fuels, no water, but instead used the constant energy exchange of charges between ions to run a modified microrocket engine. Totally impractical for anyone who didn't have more money than God. *Which I do,* Ian thought. There might have been a few other prototype ion ve-hicles on the road. Anyone who had one disguised it to look like a standard car. Best not call too much attention to what one was driving . . .

"Fewer and fewer . . ." Sam said.

"Hm?"

"Cars. Every time we come out here, there are fewer cars. Someday, maybe there'll be none."

"It's a changing world, Sam." Then, almost to himself: "And cars are the least of it. . . ."

Sam avoided a massive hole in the lane he was in; it looked like a bomb had landed on the road. Then he cut right, heading to the off ramp, into what was once wine country and now was as dry as a desert.

His father's compound was ten minutes away, and Ian reviewed what he was going to talk to his father about, the hard questions he needed help with. . . .

Ian Kelliher's car passed through the security gate while a bank of scanners scrutinized it for anything out of the ordinary. Ian could remember when he was a kid, his father would pull him aside, lecturing him about how they could only "get" you if you didn't think of everything. "You have to want yourself alive more than they want you dead, hmm?" Then he'd laugh as if it were some kind of joke, repeated over and over. But it was no joke for Tommy Kelliher. He believed that there was a legion of people who'd want him gone, permanently, not just deposed as head of the all-powerful UAC.

And here Tommy was, retired, safely ensconced in a fortress, still protected by an array of programmed defenses and a small army of guards, both on the grounds and inside the mansion, whose loyalty to the Kelliher family and the UAC was unshakable.

"Do you want the underground, sir?"

Ian shook his head. Below the main mansion sat a parking lot that could accommodate over fifty cars. But today was a halfway decent day, some sun, not too much pollution in the air. Why not walk up to the front door like a real human?

"We'll just park it in front, Sam."

His driver nodded as the vehicle slowed. The modified ion engines began to shut down, switching over to the battery power that was more suited for slow speeds. The car stopped.

Sam hopped out first, took a look around. Two guards at either side of the door nodded. *It's like visiting a small country,* Ian thought. Some crazed dictatorship with unlimited amounts of money and power and paranoia.

Ian got out of the car and hurried up the stone steps. The massive twin oak doors opened, and for a moment he felt like he was five years old again.

Ian sat in the house's boardroom, so curiously old-fashioned with high-backed chairs, a wooden table carved from a single tree, cut from someplace where trees this large still existed. He didn't have to wait long for his father to arrive, rolling in on a chair that had all the medical monitoring instruments of a small ICU. A pair of nurses trailed behind.

"Dad."

The word sounded odd. Tommy Kelliher had always been an amazing character, a genius, a ruthless businessman, someone who had become more important and powerful than the president. Although he didn't look too powerful now, sitting almost curled up in the chair, tubes and wires everywhere. Still, if you looked carefully at the old man's eyes, there was still something there. Something that gave even Ian Kelliher pause.

The man's lips opened, and the word was barely audible. "Ian."

Ian gave a nod to one of the nurses, and she touched the back of Ian's chair, raising the volume. The man struggled to get the word out. "To what do I . . . owe . . . this great . . . pleasure?"

Funny, Ian thought. *I'm his son, and yet he's viewing me almost like an opponent, another corporate bug to be crushed—if he had the strength.*

His father's hand were wrapped clawlike around the arms of the chair.

"Questions, Dad."

Tommy Kelliher's eyes squinted. Never exactly comfortable in the role of "Dad."

"Advice."

Tommy's lips opened. A slight delay before the words came out. "You have advisers. You pay people . . . to do that already."

Did he detect some scorn in those words? Ian had taken the UAC in bold new directions, and often merely kept his father in the loop these days. But it was *Tommy* Kelliher who had built the UAC, who had spearheaded the ion engine project, who had established the teams that would someday begin the early work on true molecular teleportation, the great secret work of the UAC.

Ian gave his father a smile. "But I want *your* advice. You might say I *need* your advice. Advisers or not."

His father's right hand opened and closed again over the chair's arm, and the chair slid a few feet closer. Right into a pool of light. The man was alive—no doubt about that—but there were probably cadavers that looked better.

"Then ask . . . your . . . questions . . ." A big pause. "Son."

Ian took a breath and began, hoping that the light in his father's eyes would be matched with insight that, for some reason, Ian Kelliher felt was required.

6

IAN KELLIHER LOOKED AT HIS FATHER'S two nurses, which Tommy immediately noticed. "Don't . . . worry. They know all my secrets anyway." The women remained just behind the chair, as if they were an imperial guard for their ancient patient.

"Okay. And I don't want to stay long. I know how all this . . . must tire you."

Tommy Kelliher didn't say anything, but just fixed his son with his eyes, the filmy pools now locked on. If there was one thing his father had, it was good instincts. Ian thought, *He'll know just how concerned I am*.

"Mars City. Everything—on paper—looks fine. The reports on the work being done, the teleportation experiments, the progress, the setbacks. But—"

The old man's tongue snaked out of his mouth. "But . . . not true?"

"Precisely. I have someone there, in the lab, working with Dr. Betruger."

Tommy Kelliher's eyes narrowed. Though Ian

knew that Betruger had been essential to the ion engine project—in fact, it was probably impossible without him—his father didn't like the scientist. Early on, his father had told Ian, *"You need to watch him. That man could be very dangerous."*

At the time, Ian thought that he could control Betruger. In fact, he thought that he could control anyone. Now? Nothing but uncertainty.

"And . . . what does your mole . . . tell you?"

Ian turned to the wooden desk, ready to bring up a holo-screen. "I can show you what—"

The old man sputtered. "No, *tell* me. I can't see . . . for shit. Use words, damn it. Remember words?"

Ian nodded. Though it looked as though his father's eyes could see just fine, he started to tell his father everything. About the reports Betruger sent, the breakthroughs in transmitting living matter across space, the small setbacks, the overall tone so optimistic. The images that Dr. Kellyn MacDonald secretly sent back to Earth showed something far more horrific than some small setbacks. Using just . . . words, Ian described some of the still-living monstrosities that appeared in the lab, the limbs sprouting from all parts of the bodies, the elongated jaws, mutated almost to the point of being another creature.

Then Ian stopped. His father hadn't moved during Ian's monologue. And now he waited for his father to say something.

"Who else . . . knows?"

"Not many. The scientists in the lab, but they are all carefully monitored. Any communication they have with Earth is carefully screened. For security reasons, of course."

"Of course."

"And I have a few trusted members on the Palo Alto team who have seen the images."

A slight nod from the old man. One of the nurses leaned forward slightly, looking at something at the back of the chair. Perhaps a slight increase in blood pressure? A bit of an uptick in heart rate?

"How are you handling . . . the situation?"

"Well, shutting down Betruger would be no easy thing to do. Even with my own team at the Palo Alto labs already getting some of the same results down here, he—"

His father's eyes widened. The voice, almost taking on some of its former power, became louder. "You've been doing those experiments *here*?"

"Some. Only to double-check Betruger. But not on the scale he's using; we've done nothing with human subjects, and we won't—"

The old man's eyes drifted away. "Anything else? Have you done anything else?"

"I've sent Campbell up to Mars, with full authority. Along with the UAC lead counsel, Elliot Swann. They're there now and will report directly back to me, then I will decide. But"—Ian took a breath—"as you say . . . I have a lot of advisers. But it's *your* advice I need."

His father still hadn't looked back, his watery eyes still gazing off into the distance. A slight grunt, an attempt to clear his throat, and then the man turned his head back. And damned if he didn't look worried. The same look Ian saw in the mirror every morning.

The one person that Ian Kelliher could trust completely began to talk. "You know . . . that you are playing God, right, Ian?"

Ian shook his head. "God? Why? I mean, this is research that your people started, that you initially approved, and I'm just—"

"Just—what? Finishing what I started? I—I voiced my concerns about this Mars City, even with the government paying—" The old man's voice rose, almost sounding strong, the Tommy Kelliher of years past. But then he began to cough, sputtering, as a nurse came around to see if there was anything she could do.

She glanced back at Ian as if to say, *Do you really have to have this conversation with your father now?*

Too bad. "Mars City was always part of the UAC vision."

Tommy Kelliher nodded, taking care now. "For defense, for a community, but as a mammoth secret lab?" He shook his head. "No, that was all *you.*"

"The team felt that the full range of experiments couldn't be done on Earth."

"Couldn't—or shouldn't? And now, you don't know what Betruger has done—or is still doing—up there. Even your mole may only know half of it." He paused. "I never got into a situation where I wasn't in control, where I didn't know everything. But you have."

"And the dangers?"

Ian's father smiled a bit at that. "For me, not much. How long do I have, even with all this—" He waved a hand at the back of his mobile medical center. "But this planet, the people? Despite everything, the UAC was never just about profit or power. It was about doing something for humanity. But . . . what is this? What is it you're doing? What are the dangers, you ask?"

"Yes."

"You, my son, are trifling with forces that even our best scientists don't understand. Our most brilliant physicists . . . they're like babies, playing with these things. And it could be . . . *could be* . . . there are some doors that you open, that won't close again."

At that moment, Ian knew that his father—for all his age, for all his talk of being so close to death—had his own network of loyal spies who had shared everything that Ian had seen.

Ian licked his lips. "So—what should I do?"

His father looked away again, as if some ghost in the corner might have an answer. Then he started talking without looking back. "You've gone there yourself?"

"Yes, last year."

His father looked up. "I heard you had . . . an accident?"

Ian smiled, betraying nothing. *Jesus, he knows about that, too.* "Someone went buggy. Fired a gun. Flesh wound. Nothing too big."

"Not too big, eh? The wound—or the fact that someone snapped? And maybe more have 'snapped' since then?"

"It is . . . a problem. Not too sure what's going on there."

"You have Campbell there now? That's good. And your lawyer—"

"Elliot Swann."

"He'll at least be able to deal with damage control, if needed. But—where is the Armada?"

The Armada?

Ian had to wonder why his father was asking about that. Like most of the off-Earth operations, the Armada was a joint US and UAC venture. Technology and the actual engineering of the ships themselves—that all came from the UAC, while the staffing and most of the financing came from the government. The six interplanetary ships of various sizes patrolled the solar system, ostensibly for scientific and exploratory purposes. But they also served notice on any countries who imagined that the UAC didn't control space as well.

"The Armada is near Jupiter, and there is one small cruiser, the *Centauri*, in exploratory orbit above Europa. We have—"

"Call them back."

"What?"

"You want them closer. To Mars. Leave that one ship near Europa, but the other ships should prepare to rendezvous closer to Mars and Earth."

"That will raise questions."

"So? You . . . you need to answer questions? Since when?"

Ian nodded. He could send an order through the military command in Colorado. The President would haul out the rubber stamp, not daring to question the move at all. The military high command might want to balk, but would they have the balls?

"Just get the Armada closer, Ian. Until you find out what's really going on . . . on Mars. Until you have your final reports. If you have to shut down the labs, if you have to remove people, if you have to make sure no one talks—you can't leave that to Hayden and a few squads of space marines."

"So, in other words, make it seem like something routine. An exercise of some kind." He took a breath. Then Ian Kelliher stood up in the great room. "I best get back." He took a few steps away from the table, then turned around. "Thank you. And stay well—"

"One more thing."

"Yes."

"What about . . . Ballard?"

The undersea lab? Why was his father asking

about that? "Nothing much new there. They continue their experiments, both those that are for public knowledge, and those that are not. But—"

His father raised his right hand, levitating it with difficulty from the armrest of the chair, a single finger pointing.

"There is something important there, Ian. Something that may be an even bigger secret . . . than what you have found with these experiments on Mars."

"How do you know that? They haven't—"

"Know? I don't *know* it. But I do still have my instincts. The same ones—" Another barrage of coughs. His father waited. Then: "The same ones that led to the creation of the UAC. There is something ancient there. Don't just forget them. Make sure that work continues. What that work tells you, you may need."

And here Ian had been about to pull the plug on Ballard. "Right. Guess we can afford to let them continue."

His father's hand came down and pushed a button, and the chair rolled closer until father and son faced each other, inches away. A strange smell emanated from the man in the chair—the chemicals, the medicine, the aging flesh.

"You can't afford not to, Ian. Do you understand?"

"I do."

And then without so much as a nod, or even a

good-bye, Tommy Kelliher pivoted his chair and rolled away, back into the recesses of the mansion, the two nurses dutifully following.

Ian hurried out of the room, out of the fortress-like mansion, out to fresh air and his car, waiting to take him back to Palo Alto.

2145

ARMAGEDDON

7

PRIVATE JOHN KANE ALLOWED HIS EYES TO close.

For a moment, the bright lights of Mars City Reception, now up to full power, faded a bit. He heard the steps of people moving about, some hurrying to their quarters, perhaps to hide, some looking for friends and colleagues—most of whom would likely never be seen again.

And hovering in the back, the slow heaving and sobbing of the receptionist. Kane had only seconds ago informed her that her friend who had stepped away for a few minutes would not be stepping back.

Then there were the smells. Of course the familiar—to Kane at least—smell of gunpowder, smoke, and blood—a heady mix that, once inhaled, was never forgotten. Not even the areas where people had "lost it," tossing their cookies at the bloodshed, could cut through that smell. It was primal, powerful, and—though a familiar one—he never got used to it.

Then the sounds and smells started to recede as Kane felt all the aches in his body pulling at him, tugging him into some dark hole that threatened to envelop him.

The lights were now piercingly bright, the physical signs of the mayhem that had occurred there. He saw three other grunts starting to head in the direction of the marine barracks. Kane stood up, thinking he had to get to the infirmary and get some stimulants. This was just too damn hard.

But first . . .

"Hey, you guys! Where do you think you're going?"

One of the marines, a private first class, stopped and shook his head at him. "What the hell business is it of yours"—he looked at Kane's name tag—"Kane?"

Another marine spoke up. "We're getting the hell out of here. Who knows what's happening"—and here he pointed—"thataway."

Kane nodded. Too true. Having gone in search of the missing receptionist and found—what?—some creature that walked like a dog but whose head opened up like an exploded basketball to reveal rows of teeth instead of a hollow center, he knew they had a point.

But orders were orders, and Sergeant Kelly had told them to secure this area. And a good decision that was, too. Mars City Reception was a central hub, where a number of wings of the sprawling lab and work areas came together. People would gravitate here, looking for protection, help, something. And if the marines weren't here for protection, then what the hell were they here for?

"We have orders. To secure this area, to keep—"

"Fuck that, man. Until I know what the hell's going on, this 'area' can secure itself."

Kane had moved a few feet into their path, not necessarily a hostile move, but certainly something they'd have to go around—or through—if they were going to get to their barracks. Not the first time Kane had faced nervous troops. Even rebellious troops. In the nasty wars that were waged all over planet Earth these days, such things were common.

But that was when he was still a lieutenant, before he disobeyed a direct order in Terekstan and tried to save some marines that Central Command had decided were politically expendable.

Still, lieutenant or no, Kane wasn't sure in the next few hours, or days, if rank would mean much up here. "We have an order, and we're going to follow it."

One of the grunts in front of Kane kept walking to the side of him, muttering to himself, hurrying—and not doing a terribly good job of hiding his fear. He passed on Kane's left. Kane shot his arm out. He felt the sting of the gouges and scratches that he'd received without even being aware of them—scars from his nightmare journey from the old Comm Center and the bowels of Mars City, back to here.

Still his arm moved, obeying the brain's instruction. As did his hand as it locked pincerlike around the man's throat.

At the same time he saw the other two space marines start moving their weapons.

His left hand closed just a bit around the man's windpipe.

"One little squeeze, and you're dead. No discussion, no more orders to follow, and"—he looked at the other two with their weapons nearly at the ready position—"if you two idiots decide to actually point those weapons, then he'll get to see me blow holes in you so fast that, well, on the plus side, you won't even know what the hell hit you."

The weapons stopped in mid-motion.

"Good. Everyone listen real well now, and I'll tell you what *will* happen. You will get back to patrolling your perimeter." Kane pointed to a hallway leading off the far end of Reception. "Two of you take one way, one go the other. Meet in the middle. Oh—and I don't give a damn who gets left on his own."

Kane released his hold on the marine's throat. The young grunt coughed, gulping at the air.

"You check in with me every ten minutes or so. I don't hear from you, then I think something bad has happened." Kane took a breath. *This*, he thought, *was almost fun*. "But that 'bad' thing better not be that you found another way to leave your post."

One of the marines, a taller one who looked as though he might still be evaluating some resistance to Kane, took a step forward. *At least the muzzle of his gun is down*, Kane noticed.

"Why should we take orders from you?"

Kane looked at him. This marine might be an ally if things kicked in again. Soldiers had many sides, from the craven to the heroic, and the person who led them had to know all about that.

"Two reasons: First, Kelly asked *me* to get things under control here. And until someone shows up who outranks me"—Kane looked at the two stripes on the other private's arm—"*really* outranks me, then that is exactly what the hell I'm going to do."

Kane looked around Reception. A sense of stillness filled the area. The few civilian workers consoling themselves, a few other marines standing on guard but also looking at this scene as it played out.

"But there's another reason. You see, I want to live. I want to get off this planet someday, somehow, alive. And trust me, I will do all I can to make that happen. If that means saving as many of these people as I can, then that's exactly what I will do." Another beat. "And so will you."

Then—an amazing moment—the three of them nodded. The taller grunt—Kane took a look at his name tag: *McCullough*—said to the other two rebellious marines, "Come on, let's go. We'll do the damn patrols."

They turned and headed down the hallway—where, Kane had to admit, who knew what the hell awaited them?

8

IAN KELLIHER STUDIED GENERAL HAYDEN'S face. Campbell stood to the general's right, just out of view. Kelliher could pan the camera to see Campbell, or pull back to view them both.

But for now he wanted to get a close look at the general in charge of Mars City as he tried to describe what he had just called, for the tenth or eleventh time, "the situation."

If the general was streaming bullshit from Mars down to this office on Earth, Kelliher wanted every chance to be able to detect it.

The same mechanism that allowed interplanetary travel at heretofore impossible speeds also allowed near synchronous and contemporaneous communication between Earth and Mars. Save for odd moments when a bit of delay would kick in—some random fluctuation that Kelliher's scientists had not been able to eradicate. Something to do with the solar winds was their latest theory.

Hayden's face, lined, overly bronze from the officers' spa and the artificial sun, told Kelliher a lot of what he needed to know. The military bastard was scared.

"So, General, there are still sectors where you are not getting any information?"

A pause, and this time it had nothing to do with solar winds. Then: "All the units have checked in with their status, and the situation—"

That damn word again. . . .

"—reported is that all areas are under control."

Hayden blinked. A leathery-looking tongue snaked out and took a stab at wetting his lips, but to no avail.

Scared, and he isn't telling me everything. And maybe he isn't telling me everything because he just doesn't know.

Kelliher touched the keyboard floating like a lamp to his right, and the camera pulled back to show Campbell standing beside Hayden. Kelliher had questions for him.

"General, I want to ask you a question and it's very important that you give me as truthful an answer as you can. Do you understand?" *Like talking to some goddamn kid.*

"Yes, of course. I wouldn't do anything but—"

"So again: Are there sectors of Mars City that you currently have no information about, places where you don't know what the 'situation' might be? And if so, what are those places?"

Again Hayden looked away, gathering his thoughts. The fact that Campbell stood beside him—Kelliher's own man sent up to assist Elliot Swann with his evaluation of the whole Mars City operation—might force Hayden to be honest. If nothing else, it felt good to watch the general squirm.

"We know that Alpha Lab is secure. We have taken losses there—heavy losses. But it is secure. . . ."

Kelliher also wanted to review the security vid with Hayden to get a handle on what might have happened, or what might still be happening. But that could wait for now. . . .

"And I have had a marine return from the lower section leading to Old Communications. As far as we can tell, that is now clear. But there are so many chambers, tunnels, down there, it's hard—"

"Go on."

"The monorail station, and the pods connected to it, all look quiet. The reception area and loading bays are all fine. The main access points to the exterior also report nothing happening. Further, the Hydrocons have all been checked, with new guard units there, and—"

Enough of this crap, Kelliher thought.

"Delta, General. Delta. I do hope you haven't forgotten about the area in which I have invested an amazing amount of the UAC's resources for the past ten years?"

Kelliher panned the camera up and over to Campbell. There was no way that anyone in the room could tell that Kelliher was jumping around, zeroing in here and there, pulling back. But he imagined that Jack Campbell, who knew Ian Kelliher about as well as anyone, would assume that Kelliher was studying his face for some reaction to Hayden's dodging of the big question. . . .

What the hell is happening in Delta?

Hayden shifted in his seat, nodded.

"Yes. Delta. I—I was get—" The communication system hiccoughed, and Hayden's nervous words were further stilted by the tiny breakup.

"—ting to that. Delta. It's an area . . . an area of some concern."

Hayden waited a moment. The general probably hoped there would be questions, but Kelliher wanted him to speak, wanted to keep him roasting.

9

PRIVATE MARIA MORAETES LOOKED AT WHAT was left of the squad as Andy Kim came to her side. "Bad news, Maria. No one left here who outranks you. There is one guy"—Kim turned away so his words couldn't be detected—"that has some more bars, even an Earth-side battle ribbon. But from the look in his eyes, I wouldn't bother knocking on that door."

"Great. So you're saying there is no one here to run this outfit?"

Kim smiled. "No one except you."

They both looked back toward Alpha, where Deuce had been ripped to shreds before their eyes as if they lived in some crazy vid, a game where such things could happen, Except they could do nothing but stand there as his skin opened up like ripe fruit and blood sprayed the hallway like a painter gone mad. . . .

There were a dozen or so soldiers milling about, all appearing as if they had just awakened to the sickest nightmare of their lives. Not good, she told herself. She turned back to Kim. "Look, Andy, we have to get these guys back into patrols, into some kind of formation. Just—just standing here isn't working."

Andy Kim licked his lips and his eyes darted from the group and back to her. And she knew that Andy too might be in a place inside his own head that he'd never dreamed about. But if Kim should fall apart, that would really leave her alone. *And what's holding me together?* she wondered.

"Okay, fine, here's what I'm going to do," she said. "Get them into some kind of grouping, get a patrol to head back to Alpha—"

Kim's eyes widened. Not going to be an easy task, that.

"Don't worry," she added quickly, "I'll take the lead on that."

Kim nodded.

"You start a patrol here. We've got—what?—three different areas converging. Some kind of regular patrols. And listen—we check in every five minutes, got that?"

"Okay," he said quietly.

"And lastly, we leave a few guards here. They can see all three paths, got a really good view. And again, they can check in every five minutes too."

Maria knew which post she'd want if she had her choice: staying right here, gun at the ready, looking down those long hallways to see what might be coming.

Kim cleared his throat. "How's everyone's ammo?"

"Good point. Best to check. Everyone was firing as if the goddamn supply was endless."

"And if low?"

Now Maria took a breath. "Okay, um, we have to send someone to get some ammo."

"I guess so."

"All right, no point in waiting. Let's start talking to them."

Maria turned to the grunts, mostly men, but including two women, who stood to the side, and started walking to them.

"Hold on, hold on—just listen, and—"

One of the group turned to the others. "We should stay the hell here! Until we get orders. Until we hear from Sarge, or someone"—he looked right back at Maria—"with some bars on their shoulder."

"Listen," Maria said, making her voice as loud as possible without yelling, without sounding as if she had edged just a bit closer to losing it. "You know that sooner or later they *will* give us some orders. But if they hear we've been standing around as if we were waiting for a bus, well"—she looked at the soldier who had emerged as her most vocal opponent—"you try explaining that. And if people die because we were all here hiding, cowering—"

Fighting words, she knew, to any marine, whether a space marine or the more earthly variety.

"—you can be sure that, as bad as this is, for some of us it could get a lot worse."

"At least we'd still be alive."

Another voice. Perhaps the ringleader's side-kick. Might be a good pressure point to hit, Maria thought. And if she knew anything from her years as a marine, and before that her years in a ring trading blows with some other woman equally eager to take her down, it was to look for the pressure points, places where the right move could expose a weakness.

"Really? Is that what we are all about now? Staying alive? Well, I got a news flash for you, Private, that's what I want to do, too. Except I don't think hiding here is the way to do it. I think that we should set up a perimeter. I think we need to know if anything might still be out there, closing in on us. You see, I think we stand"—another step toward the soldier, whose height had him eyeball-to-eyeball with her—"a damn sight better chance if we act like goddamn soldiers rather than a bunch of old ladies . . ."

She added a bit of a sneer for effect.

". . . or old men." Now she looked around at the others. She felt Kim's eyes on her, waiting to see how this was going to go down. Otherwise, it would be the two of them, alone. About as bad odds as there could be.

"What do you say?" She directed the question to the group, but no one answered her.

"Okay, good. I'm no officer but I can get us orga-
nized to—I dunno—what do you call it?" She smiled
now, the tension easing. " 'Secure' the area."

Kim came and stood by her.

"Okay, we're going to need three groups. One to
head back to Alpha—" She brought the toughest
one up first, and quickly added, "Which I will lead.
One to start a patrol of this intersection, down the
hallways, back. Constant radio contact. Every five
minutes we check in. And then a few grunts to stay
here, but weapons at the ready in case whatever the
hell happened starts happening again. Any questions?"

Suddenly, the scared and rebellious group were
soldiers again. And Maria thought, *If I hadn't screwed
up my career by trying to save the UAC boss from a crazy
grunt's bullet six months ago, I might have made a damn
good officer.*

"Good. Well, I have one. Can we check ammo?
Everyone. Let me know what you got. Because if
we're low . . ." She let the words trail off. They might
need a fourth group to solve the ammo supply problem. And everyone there knew how far away that
section was.

10

THEO PULLED HIS KNEES UP TO HIS CHEST AS tight as he could, the hard bone of his jaw against his kneecap. For some reason—he didn't know why—he banged his chin against his knee once, twice, a third time, and—

What was that? A noise, somewhere down there. He felt himself start to breathe again in that funny way, taking the air in fast, as if he were in some kind of race. He tried to listen to the sound of his breathing—could it be heard?

Could they hear it?

And then what? If they knew he was up here, would they stop and somehow find a way to climb up here, just as he did, and crawl into this small opening, just barely big enough for him. But then he thought: Could it be other people, like that soldier who saved him . . . saved him . . . saved him—

From his own mother.

What if soldiers came, and he sat so still that they passed right by him? And he'd be left alone again, in this dark space, the only light coming from the room below and farther down this metal tunnel?

He forced himself to pay attention to any sounds down there, and not worry about his breathing. He wished there was some way to make his ears work better. Could they be aimed if he tilted and turned? And what sounds should he listen for? The sound of steps, soldiers' boots, and the clanking of their guns? Or . . . the sound of something taking strange steps, and the horrible sound of claws, and—

He felt himself start to cry again. But he knew he couldn't do that. They'd hear him for sure, and come for him.

And whenever he thought about how he couldn't do this, that he had to come out and try to get some help, he remembered what happened. How the strange wind filled that hallway, how he hid behind a wall while something *happened* to his mother. And when he came out, and she slowly turned (and he was *so* glad to see her), he didn't know for the longest time that there was anything wrong.

Not until he could see her face, and then he knew that what was once his mother . . . had become something else. He had tried not to look at the rows of teeth from such a large mouth, the same mouth that once sang to him and asked him how he felt when he was sick. Now the jaw working up and down, his mother *(no, it's not my mother, not my mother, no—)* looking at him with eyes that were big and empty, but kept looking at Theo.

And from the fairy tales she had read to Theo, he knew what such eyes wanted, what they were for . . .

And then that soldier telling Theo to run, get out of here, now, fast, hurry—*run!* And Theo did, knowing that the soldier would then stop the thing that used to be his mother.

On the way out of that place, Theo saw other things. More soldiers, dead ones this time—at least, he thought they were dead. And then other monstrosities that he made himself not look at. Because he knew he'd just stand there, shivering, crying, shaking, and waiting for them.

So he ran.

And when he crawled into this place, and started to scurry away, it felt safe. A secret place. But he also knew that he couldn't stay here forever. Sooner or later, he'd have to move, have to come down.

He thought again of that soldier who saved his life. Theo wished he'd hear his voice again. But for now, he just listened very carefully. Waiting.

Now it was quiet . . . but there had been something before. Theo looked down the metal tunnel. Maybe it would be okay if he made a run for it? Keep moving, keep hiding, keep listening? And—

he told himself, when he felt as if he couldn't take it anymore—let himself remember what it was like down there.

He uncurled his legs, stretching out, and then, as though he were playing soldier in his old backyard on Earth, he started crawling forward.

11

IAN KELLIHER RAISED A HAND TO GENERAL Hayden. He didn't want to hear any more explanations of how "secure" Mars City was right now, how every goddamn thing was now well under control. "General, can you stop for a second—"

"I just wanted to review the situation in all—"

"I know. But I want to do something else. You see, General, I don't believe we have a lot of time to get up to speed."

"I assure you, Ian, that everything is under control. I certainly hope you haven't given orders to the Armada."

Kelliher winced at Hayden's use of his first name. "Mr. Kelliher" would be much more preferable. But then, Hayden was a bona fide hero of many of the shitty little wars of the past decades—or so his CV seemed to indicate. And having started with the precedent that Hayden was "General" and Kelliher was "Ian," it would be a bit hard to change it now.

And Hayden had just raised an interesting point in this aftermath. On Mars, it was clear who was running the operation—the UAC. Funded largely with UAC money, Mars City was mostly a corporate operation with the support, tactical and financial, of the American people. Whether they wanted it or not.

But the Armada? That was a different story. The brass in the New Pentagon would never have turned over the operation of their primary defensive and offensive space shield to a private enterprise. Sure, there was a good deal of cooperation back and forth: shared technology, resources, even money. And the Armada was at the beck and call of Kelliher and Mars City—within limits. But the bottom line was that the Armada, now on routine patrol in Jupiter space in support of the Europa expedition, remained under military control.

So what would be the implications of summoning it to Mars, to calling on it for help? Could they consider that the operation had been under civilian control for too long, with obviously disastrous effects? No matter that Kelliher's father had made the entire concept of interplanetary travel feasible. The military could do what they'd done for millennia. Just march in and take over the fleet. History was filled with such lessons.

So Hayden raised a very important point. And

the fact that the bastard was military even made the point almost more of a threat. But Kelliher had to admit, it was a good move. Maybe Hayden had more going on in his brain than Kelliher gave him credit for.

"Okay, General. Not to worry. The Armada has been thoroughly briefed that whatever happened is now under control. I believe they are making their way from Jupiter, but that was the mission plan all along." Kelliher took a breath. "No alert to them has gone out from this office."

Hayden's eyes twitched a bit. The fat-ass general was probably pleased that his little game of chess had played so well. "And none from here either, Ian. I've made sure of that." A small smile. "No need, really."

"Yes. Good. No need. Now."

"Now?"

Kelliher reached to the floating keyboard. "Time to review what happened, General. Time to look at some of the pictures we have here." Now it was Kelliher's turn to look Hayden right in the eyes. "Let's look at exactly what happened, hm? And then— well, maybe you can explain it."

"Ian, there are a lot of things here that need my—"

"Exhibit 1, General. Let's just watch the vid, okay?"

A tap in the air, then Hayden's face shrank to a box in the corner of the screen, and suddenly they had a crystal clear, breathtaking view of a section of Mars City near the lower Hydrocon units. Two space marines stood close to a wall, weapons slung over their shoulders. Kelliher brought up the audio.

"So—get this—she sent me another one. Last night. Even a hotter pic, man. I got to tell you—she's driving me crazy."

The other marine laughed. "You are one lucky son of a—"

The sound of steps, and the two marines in the vid straightened up. One looked at his PDA as if an urgent message had just come through. But when the third person entered the area, they both relaxed again.

"Carpenter? What the hell you doing here? Lost again?"

The third marine stopped. Kelliher noticed that this new entry, Carpenter, stood in the hallway. The other two were in a recessed area, so that if someone—a lieutenant or sergeant—was looking for their sorry asses, he wouldn't see them just standing there.

"Kelly gave me an order to check power levels—in person. God, can't they just—you know—look at their meters or something? Waste of my time."

One of the other marines chuckled. "And your time is so valuable, right, Carpy? That's one thing we don't want to waste."

And all three of them laughed at that. The sound was warm, human. In another second, the sound of that laughter became swamped with something else.

Instinctively, Kelliher leaned back. Hayden pre-emptively cleared his throat. "Ian, I've seen this. And—"

"Hold on, General. Indulge me."

The sound of the shock wave blew out whatever was picking up audio. Good thing, Kelliher thought, considering what was coming. The two marines curled up close to the wall, their instincts quickly taking them out of the blast of whatever the hell just roared down that hallway.

But the third marine—

He disappeared in a smoky orange-red glow. For a moment he was completely invisible, but then Kelliher could make out the outline of a shape in the haze. At the same time, the two soldiers stood up, first looking at each other, then—it seemed—as if one of them looked down at his body to make sure it was all there.

It is for now, Kelliher thought. Another few seconds, and the third soldier could be seen. Or more appropriately, what had once been a soldier. With each passing second, his image became clearer. Kelliher felt his stomach tighten. Hard to repress the gag reflex, even though he had seen this a few times.

The face was the first thing that became visible. Except, with one eye nearly bulging out of its socket, and the other recessed and floating in a pool of bloody mucous, it was hard not to look away. But the jaw truly commanded one's attention. Twice as large as a normal jaw, it snapped open and shut, its owner getting a handle on using this massive instrument. Teeth somehow jutted out sharply at all sorts of different angles.

Kelliher thought, *How the hell did that happen so fast? Or did it? Is there something involving time going on here? Could what appears to be a few seconds actually be something else?*

Only a few moments to take the rest of the creature in: hands turned into elongated claws, chunks of his uniform hanging off like some parchment blown away, exposing flesh—Kelliher imagined—below. But what flesh? The color of it now bronze and red, gashes and red lines scuttling across it. He swore he saw a new opening, oozing, just . . . appearing.

No audio. So no chance to hear what the two soldiers, now standing, looking at their friend, had to say. Probably "Holy shit." Or "Goddamn." Did they think it was really still their comrade, another space marine who happened to be standing in the wrong place at the wrong time?

"Ian, you can stop it."

But Kelliher didn't. He let it run as the creature moved with terrifying speed and precision. One would have guessed it would have—what?—lumbered, staggered, wounded, sliding toward the other soldiers. But no, it moved with the speed of a trained predator. The two clawed hands flew up, each landing on the neck of one of the other two soldiers. Kelliher looked away, just for a moment, then back to see the claws close. Then the men began gagging, their jaws open, trying to make a sound. But it was easy to see that the creature's claws had closed tight around their throats, almost enough to sever the heads from the bodies.

But not quite.

The once human thing brought one soldier to its mouth and, with that same speed, bit down on his head as if eating a candy apple. Thank God there was no sound, as it cracked right through the skull with one great bite. The creature didn't spit out the chunk.

But it did bring the other soldier, who Kelliher hoped (really, really hoped) was already dead, and did the same thing to him. And after several more bites, whatever the once-marine held in its claw-hands no longer looked like humans at all.

Kelliher reached up to the floating keyboard and killed the vid.

"Christ, Ian. Why did we have to watch that again?"

"Okay, General—can you tell me what we just saw? What the hell was that?"

"We—we're not sure. Some of the men have started to call them zombies." A nervous laugh from Hayden. He started to say something else, but again some fluctuation in the signal allowed a few seconds' delay to kick in. In a moment, the audio caught up again: "I have teams looking at it now, Ian. A disease, a virus—"

Kelliher shook his head, then said, "Hope I don't catch it."

The sick joke sat in the room for a minute. Hayden took a breath and tried to continue. "Thing is, we don't know what happened, except that it came from Delta. The good thing is—"

"Oh, there's a good thing about all this?"

"Delta has been secured. Dr. Betruger has Delta completely secure and has begun an investigation of the incident."

"Incident. I do hope you have the area sealed off."

"Of course. In fact, Betruger did that internally. But we also dispatched Sergeant Kelly and a full squad to position themselves at all the points of egress from Delta. Nothing in, nothing out, until we know what's going on."

Somehow the words didn't give Kelliher any sense of security. "So not many theories, eh? Disease? Radiation of some kind from the teleportation process? Something—whatever it is—that works fast. . . ."

Hayden said nothing.

"Any idea of how many of them there are? Your zombies."

"Not yet. We haven't begun full patrols of all of Mars City. Still securing—"

"Begin them."

"Yes, we will." Hayden looked as if he thought that their chat was done.

"Hold on, General. I know you have a lot to deal with up there, but there's one more thing I want to show you."

Hayden settled back in his chair, looking like a twelve-year-old about to see how badly he had screwed up.

"Take a look at this. If you would. As long as we're talking theories, ideas. Okay?"

Hayden nodded, and Kelliher began the second vid.

12

KANE WALKED OVER TO THE CURVED RECEPTION desk. The woman at the desk was still curled up, still heaving, sobbing, a clenched fist muffling her tears, and didn't even look up at him.

Behind her, Kane looked at the massive 3-D panorama of Mars City, a vision of the future when the labs and tunnels here would have given way to towers filled with people living here as this Red Planet supposedly—and miraculously—became terraformed back to life.

That dream seemed dead now. *Going to be mighty hard getting pioneers to come live here. Not until they get all the bodies out of the way.*

Only twenty minutes ago, Kane had gone to look for this woman's friend, the other receptionist, who found out that even a woman's restroom could suddenly turn into a trap out of her worst nightmares.

He leaned down. "Anything I can do?" He glanced at her name tag. "Molly? Can I get you anything?"

She looked up, her eyes wracked by her nonstop crying. She shook her head.

"Would you want to go back to your quarters and—"

Kane barely had time to get the question out before she began violently shaking her head.

"Okay, okay. You can stay right here." He imagined that the thought of going back there, probably alone, only terrified her more. At least there were soldiers here, and guns, and lots of light. Not that any of that gave Kane a feeling of security. He straightened up and turned to one of the nearby guards, a woman. "You—come over here." The marine walked over, and Kane noticed that no one seemed to question any orders he gave. Must be something to do with the voice, he thought. Once a squad leader, always a squad leader. "I want you to take a position here. By the desk." He looked down at the receptionist. "Keep your eyes peeled in either direction, but stay here, got it?"

"Yes, s—"

The marine, a private just like Kane, had almost said "sir." Kane smiled, and he saw that she smiled back. "Good."

Kane walked away from the desk. Everything was quiet here. And as he knew too well from leading troops into so many dark and quiet streets, that could be a sign that the worst was yet to come.

He touched the send button of his wireless transmitter. Time to find out what the hell he should do now. "Sergeant Kelly? Kane here."

Nothing. Kane licked his lips. He had to get some water soon.

"Sergeant Kelly?"

Then an old-fashioned crackle—a sound from the dawn of electronic communications—and he heard Kelly's voice. "Yeah, Kane. What the hell is it?"

"I'm just checking in, Sergeant. Everything looks quiet here. I've started some patrols. Are you bringing your men back?"

More crackling sounds. Then he heard Kelly yelling something barely intelligible, a command, barked, frantic. "Yeah—goddamn it—get those men back here now!" Another order for someone on-site outside Delta Lab. "Kane, we're getting some readings inside. Some signatures indicating—jeez—I don't know. But there's something still going on inside, like maybe some troops came in from the north entrance."

"Did you have a patrol there?"

"No. The only patrol I had there had been sent to Site 3. Maybe the meters are wrong. Goddamn technology."

"Maybe you should go in?" Once again Kane realized that though Kelly was his chief, now he was giving the sergeant advice.

"Betruger has the place locked up tight. Everything's okay, he says. But still—shit."

"Did you check in with Hayden, or your lieutenant?"

"Lieutenant's dead. Got that news just a few minutes ago. And Hayden—guess he's talking to Earth. Damn—what the hell?"

"What is it?"

"Another spike, this time the energy levels inside. What the hell is he doing in there?"

"Radiation? Maybe you—"

"Look, Kane, I have to get the men here into position. If Betruger doesn't open up Delta soon, we're going in. You're on top of things there, right? Everything okay?"

The bastard sounds scared, thought Kane. *Never good to make decisions when you're scared. Fear can be the great and final fuckup.* "Yeah, I'm okay. I'll check in."

"Right, yeah—"

Then Kelly cut the communication. Kane looked around Reception. *Like we're all waiting for something here,* Kane thought. *So patiently waiting . . .*

He walked over to the young marine standing by the reception desk. "I'm going to have a look around. You okay here?"

He could see that the woman probably wanted to say "Hell, no." But she nodded. "Good. I will check back with you. But there's somebody I'd like to look for. I shouldn't be gone for long. Twenty minutes max. Anything happens"—he tapped his earpiece—"just let me know."

"Yes, Kane."

There, that sounded better. After all that Kane had been through—the court-martial for disobeying orders to save marines, then being bounced down to private, sent to Mars—a "sir" now just wouldn't sound right.

"Good. Twenty minutes, and I'm back."

He turned and started down the hall leading to the elevators that went to the lower levels of Mars City.

One of the elevators looked completely out of commission—filled with bloody smears and dozens of bullet holes that peppered the walls and ceiling. Looked like whatever had come here had taken the passenger away.

But the second elevator worked. The ID system picked up Kane's tag. With all the systems back on line, the security locks were engaged. Which actually could be a problem. Might be something he'd mention to Kelly. For now, he would deactivate the security locks so people could have easy access to whatever damn hallway they wanted to use.

The elevator's doors opened.

He took a breath. The smell hit him immediately. Blood, heavy and metallic. But something else, too: a completely unfamiliar smell that made his stomach wrench.

He took a few steps into the elevator as the door slowly closed behind him. The car plunged down to the floor just below Reception.

Kane tensed as the elevator doors slid slowly open. He took a tentative step out.

"Hello," he called. The empty corridor swallowed the sound. He called again, louder: "Hello?"

He stood stock-still. Was there no one alive down here? Then a noise. A scraping sound. Movement, but far away.

His machine gun had been over his shoulder, but now he slowly brought it around, the muzzle facing down. Kane tried to get his bearings. Where had he seen that kid and his mother? What direction did the kid run? Then he thought that surely the boy must have run into someone or something else. Either some marines who would have taken him up top to the barracks for safety . . .

Or something that used to be a marine.

Kane rubbed his throat. Like whatever that eight-foot-tall thing was that had grabbed Kane, lifting him like he was filled with helium.

"Hey, you there?" he said again, his voice echoing in the metal hallway. He thought of heading back to Reception. Being down here alone was a little much, even for him. But it wouldn't hurt to do a quick scan to make sure that somehow the boy wasn't still here.

The sound of his steps adding to the eerie gloom, Kane started his patrol.

He turned to the right and stopped. He lifted up his PDA, continually tracking his progress in the complex. He had just entered an area that he hadn't seen before. Massive cylinders lined the right wall. Gliding his finger over that area on the PDA map revealed them to be part of the Energy Processing System, whatever the hell that was.

Enough, he thought. Time to head back.

Kelly could tell him about the security system down here. There had to be some heat/motion detection system. If there was a small boy running around, hiding, terrified, it had to show up somewhere. But walking around like this and looking? Pointless. One good thing was that there seemed to be nothing down here. Nothing alive, at least. He had forced himself to ignore the bodies he passed, or what were once bodies. Some had been ripped apart, eviscerated, turned into red, sodden piles.

Gonna be a hell of cleanup job, he thought. *Probably I'll be one of the grunts to do it.*

The PDA map turned as he did, now showing the way back to the main elevator and the comparative sanity above. Which was when the radio came to life in his ear. And as a testament to how jumpy he felt, he had to take a breath before answering. "Yeah?"

"Kane? Maria here. Where the hell are you? What are you doing?"

"Taking a little walk." A little humor. Could always be good in cutting the tension. The worse things got, the more you needed the small joke. Except, down here, it didn't feel as though it were going to be too effective.

"Yeah, sorry—I'm looking for a kid I saw down here. His mother . . . turned into one of those things. Then he ran away."

Kane told the kid to run, run as fast as he could. And when the kid was out of sight, Kane killed the thing that used to be the boy's mother.

"'Turned'? Is that the expression we're using? When people become those things?"

"I dunno, Maria. What would you call it?"

He wanted to ask her then if she had seen . . . other things. Like the monsters that he had seen in his trek back to Reception. But he didn't ask her, figuring that if she had seen something, she'd tell him. And if she hadn't, why give her something else to worry about.

"Everything okay by Alpha?"

"Yes, I mean, I got some patrols running, checking in with me. Could use some real brass running things."

"You're doing fine."

"And you?" she asked. "How are things by Reception?"

"Had a little rebellion a few minutes ago. But put that down. Amazing what the threat of pain can do."

"And Kelly?"

"He hasn't checked in with you?"

He heard Maria hesitate. "No, I mean, I tried contacting him, but I got a burst of static back that nearly blew my eardrums."

"Yeah, there's some transmission problems by Delta."

"But you . . . you have heard from him?"

"Yes. He sounded a little . . . stressed."

Another hesitation. Kane didn't want to alarm Maria. But there was a big difference between the idea of alarm and alerting someone.

"But I thought everything was secure."

Kane explained about Kelly's last message, the readings coming from within Delta, his deployment of his squad there.

"I don't like it," she said.

"Me either." Kane looked around, creeped out. Too damn quiet. Before, he had moved through this area fueled on pure adrenaline. Now, in the silence, the cool, dark aftermath, it all started to get to him, to worm into that primal part of his mind, reminding him that cave people used to huddle before a fire, shivering and terrified, as unknown danger lurked all around them in the gloom.

"Maybe," he said, "you should bring some of the marines back. Be good to start getting a count, a handle on our numbers."

"And leave some patrols?"

"Yeah. They won't be happy. Tell them Kelly ordered it."

"In other words, lie."

Kane laughed. "Exactly. Then we can see what kind of numbers we have on our end. Weapons. Might need to do some ammo runs too."

"That's already on my mind. Let me wait until I have everyone back here. Maybe we can meet up."

That thought somehow made Kane feel about as

good as he could down here. "Great. Let me know where." He thought of the path back from Alpha. Was it clear? Should he send some marines to meet her halfway? Who knew what was hiding on the way back from Alpha?

"You got it. Stay safe." The radio went dead.

Kane started moving fast down the corridor, his left leg delivering a spike of pain with each step. *Meds,* he thought, *need meds. Shut off the damn pain. Got to grab a few stim packs. And who knows when there will be a time to sleep.*

Don't even go there, he told himself. *Don't even let yourself think about* that.

He followed the curving wall while the energy cylinders to his right gave way to a nest of exposed pipes and tubes. He looked down at his PDA . . . then came to a halt.

Because something had stepped out right in front of him.

13

KANE COULD BARELY MAKE OUT THE SHAPES in front of him. If he hadn't lived through the past hours he might have thought, *Dogs. There are three dogs in front of me. Cutting me off.*

But he could be sure that they weren't dogs. Even in the half-light he could see that they looked like the things he had blown to pieces in the restroom above. He didn't ask himself what they were then, and he wasn't going to now.

One of the creatures moved to the side. He saw another look back as if considering moving in another direction. Which is when the third one leaped at him.

The creature's powerful hind legs sent it—so big and bulky—flying right at him. More of the animal came into the light, and Kane could see the head. A gaping hole filled with teeth. Bits of something hanging from the teeth. These three had obviously been having a great time down here, feasting.

Kane's finger tightened on the trigger, sending a spray of bullets at the thing leaping toward him. *Enough to kill it?* he wondered. He tried to move to the side but could gain only inches before the weight of the thing sent him flying backward. As he hit the hard ground, the dog-thing's face now in his face, he heard the sickening noise of claws on stone. *The other two moving.*

Kane tried not to breathe, not with the thing in his face. But the weight of the creature had knocked the wind out of him, and he had to gasp. The smell, the taste of air, made him gag. Each breath made him hack and cough. There was nothing he had ever smelled that came close. Not in all the carnage he had seen in his years as a marine.

The sound of clawed feet came closer as the other two positioned themselves to pounce upon the pinned Kane.

He had to get out from under the thing. And it could only be a random guess if that side was safer.

The creature barely slid off him. But the skin was just slimy enough so he could roll out from under it, and then Kane quickly scrambled back to his feet.

One of the creatures closed its jaw on his right boot. No way regulation boot leather could withstand the pressure. In a second his foot would be crushed by the viselike maw. He aimed down and fired his gun right at the creature's misshapen eyes, one larger and protruding, either the result of a wound or maybe because that's how they made them up here.

One eye looking like some misbegotten egg, the other floating free as if detached from whatever passed for a brain in the creature. But his gun riveted a dozen holes in the head, and the jaw loosened, just as Kane felt the pressure on his instep.

Wouldn't have been good losing the ability to walk. Might be a useful skill to have up here.

There was still one more thing ready to fight. Kane turned to see that it was distracted momentarily, taking a big bite out of its fallen brother. *Guess they don't much care where the meat comes from.* It ripped a chunk out of the exposed belly of the first dead creature, and then, still chewing, clambered over it to come at Kane.

Kane pulled the trigger.

Nothing. Out of ammo. And no small sidearm to whip out.

The thing, as if sensing Kane's state, spit out what it was chewing and dug its claws deep into the dead body for traction. Kane kicked back, and braced himself for the attack.

Kane had his back to the wall—and the meaning of that expression never seemed clearer. There was nowhere for him to go, and with no ammo, he had only one choice. Go hand to claw with this creature.

He spoke to himself, if only to cover the sick

grunting noises the thing made. "Come on, you ugly bastard." A last deep breath, then he yelled: "Come on!"

The words had no effect on the creature, but as Kane pushed against the wall, he brought his gun as tight to his body as he could. He had to time the next move perfectly, because he knew he'd get only one chance.

In a moment the thing would be on him, pinning him and chomping down.

Inches away, the smell wafting over, the stench of the creature's breath, the aroma of partially chewed flesh.

Another second—and—

He made the muzzle of his gun fly forward with all the speed and the strength he had. He doubted if he had ever made a single move in his entire life that was this important.

If he missed, the muzzle would hit the hard helmetlike shell of the dog-like monster.

He had a moment's hesitation while he wavered in his decision: which eye to target? The left one, bigger, bulbous? Or the right eye, smaller, but maybe closer to whatever this thing used to think and move. He chose the left—bigger target, less chance of missing—and hoped that the eye responded as an ordinary eye would if a gun muzzle was jammed into it.

His aim looked good. The creature moved toward him with a steady, head-bobbing movement. That made it a moving target, but at least there was a pattern, down up, down up, and probably looking to make its fatal bite on the downswing of the head.

The muzzle in motion—

His arms were at a bad angle because he was pressed against the wall, cramped.

And though it was just one fast move, like all such moments it seemed to happen so slowly.

Until he knew he was going to miss. Maybe the timing was bad, or maybe the creature moved to the side—but he'd miss it by millimeters.

Which is when the creature tilted its head, the jaw dropping open like the mammoth metal maw of a compactor ready to devour a few tons of metal.

And in the move, the thing magically put his muzzle on target again.

Kane watched the muzzle plunge into the eye. At first no resistance, then something bony and hard.

But the move stopped the creature, and now Kane used the muzzle like a fork, turning and twisting it, until somehow it pushed deeper into the opening. The thing tried to pull back, but Kane pressed his advantage.

"You . . . big . . . smelly . . . bastard . . ."

He pressed down against the thing as hard as he could. It made a moaning sound, a low pitiful rumbling noise.

More pressure, and Kane now had a good angle, still pushing hard, driving the thing back as it shook its head furiously right and left, trying to lose the thing embedded in its head. No way *that* was happening.

Kane noticed—as if hearing it coming from some other universe—his own voice, yelling, screaming at the thing. Just a word, then another, his own grunts matched to what he hoped were the death grunts of the thing.

Yeah, It can feel pain. It can die. For now that was all the information he needed. Until he felt the thing hit the dead body of its brother creature and roll over, the jaw flopped open, useless. No more bites for this one. He waited until he was sure that the thing had no more life left in it. And only then did he slowly withdraw the gun, the end dripping with stuff from within the creature's head.

He scraped the muzzle on the carcass of the creature, rubbing it off as best he could. He should get a new gun, soon as he could. Otherwise he'd walk around smelling like the insides of one of these things.

But for now—even without ammo—he'd keep this one. Even with no bullets, it turned out to be a mighty handy thing to have.

He started back to the elevators and the comparative sanity of the upper level of Mars City.

14

"YOU'RE STILL WATCHING THIS, GENERAL?"

"Yes, Ian. I've seen these, and I—"

Kelliher held up a hand. "Just wait."

The vid now showed three marines squared off against what looked to be easily double that number of what used to be human. Single shots didn't do anything, though the lighting was good enough that Kelliher could see—yet again—how the shots ripped holes into the attackers' bodies, and something spilled out. Didn't look exactly like blood. There was a reddish tint to some of it, but it was almost violet, blackish.

Kelliher froze the image. "So, General—you see how little damage the bullets do?"

"Unless those things are carefully targeted, yes, Ian. We know that now."

"But here's my big question, General Hayden.

How could whatever happened change their body chemistry so quickly that they no longer even *bleed?* So that now something else comes out of these things, as you call them."

"We won't know, Ian. Not until we get into Delta."

"And when will you do that?"

"We're still waiting on Dr. Betruger."

Kelliher watched Hayden's sick-looking face. *The man is way over his head,* Kelliher thought. A massive enterprise like Mars City, maybe the single most important endeavor in the history of mankind, and it was all falling apart.

Kelliher started the vid again. And now a zombie reached one of the shooting marines and leaped on him, biting down on his neck. There, at least, was real blood. But the other marines finally caught on to the fact that headshots might be more effective and started blasting away.

Zombie marines began reaching up to the newly opened holes in their heads, then a moment's confused realization before they stumbled forward and fell to the around.

When just two surviving marines stood there, the corridor filled with gun smoke. Then in the quiet Kelliher heard something that he had missed the first time. One of the men was crying.

He stopped the vid.

"Okay. Some of your men have been turned into those things. We get that—even if we don't know how. Then, there's this."

A different creature now filled the screen. Tall, with raptorlike feet, hands raised in a permanent attack position, and an angular snakelike head and sharp, pointed ears that twitched as it stood there.

"Guess we don't have any vids of one of *these* being killed."

"We have dispatched some," Hayden said quietly.

"It's obviously not an infected marine. Did they come from Delta, General? Or . . . maybe not?"

"We need more information about them."

"Right." Kelliher took a breath. What a clusterfuck.

"Some men are calling them demons. Some of the more superstitious ones. Others are calling them imps. Something—I guess—about the ears."

"Doesn't look too much like any goddamn imp, General. But you know what? I sure like that name a whole hell of a lot better than 'demon.'"

Hayden said nothing.

"And this? We've only received one image down here."

The screen caught a doglike animal cornered, taking multiple shots, but still with a grisly chunk of something gripped tight in its incredible maw.

"Am I correct, General, that this thing's hindquarters appear to be . . . mechanical?"

Another throat clearing from Hayden. If Kelliher had any other candidate for command of Mars City, he'd put him in charge immediately.

"They appear to be, Ian. Looks like stuff that may

have been part of the structure of Delta. In the blast, perhaps, something maybe—"

Kelliher cut him off. "Don't worry, Hayden. I don't really expect you to explain how that thing came about. And you are calling them—"

"Pinkies."

Kelliher laughed. *Pinkies,* due no doubt to the rose color of their front section. And he also recognized that the names—so far—were all designed to minimize the opponent. Classic military double-think. Ridicule and minimize the enemy. *Good luck with that plan,* Kelliher thought. "Okay. And that's it so far?"

"Yes."

"And the status of Delta now?"

"Betruger says all is quiet there. He sealed it after the first explosions. He started doing a catastrophe analysis. He says they are assessing damage, and—"

Kelliher interrupted. "It's all buttoned up?"

"Yes."

"And when are you opening it again?"

"As I mentioned, Ian, we are waiting for Betruger. I have Sergeant Kelly and a large force positioned at the main entrance. To secure the whole area once it's open."

"General, the time for that is *now*. You have to get in there. We have no vid, no data coming out of Delta. Anything could be happening."

"Dr. Betruger didn't think—"

"Find him. I want to speak with Betruger immediately. Convey that order to Kelly. Now."

"Yes."

The signal skipped a bit, and Hayden's affirmative seemed to elongate into a distorted version of the word, sounding almost ghostly. Kelliher was done, but now Hayden had a question.

"Ian, the Armada . . . do you think they could—"

"The Armada is of course standing by, General. But you know as well as I do that if we ask for their assistance, Mars City would no longer be under UAC control. So we will wait to do that until after you have assessed the situation in Delta—and I have spoken to Betruger."

Hayden nodded.

"Good luck, General." *You're sure as hell going to need it.*

He killed the signal to Mars.

Kelliher called in Karla, his assistant. A stunning brunette, she also happened to be one of the brightest people on his team. That said, he had made a point of not trying to become involved with her— that much intelligence, even in someone so incredibly beautiful, was not to be wasted.

"Karla, I wonder if you could so something. Keep it between us, if you would."

"Yes, sir."

"The Ballard lab. I want to speak with them, but I don't want anyone else to know it. So nothing on any communication logs, and tell them that they need to have everything completely secure at their end."

"Yes, Mr. Kelliher. And who would you like on the call?"

"Just two people—David Rodriguez and Julie Chao."

"Full video link?"

"Absolutely." Some things one had to see to believe, Kelliher knew. And what he was going to show them definitely fell into that category. "Let me know as soon as they are in place."

15

DAVID NOTICED THAT KELLIHER LOOKED TO the side while the last vid played. Then, slowly, Kelliher filled the whole screen. And he said only one word: "Well?"

David took a breath. As project leader of the undersea lab, if there was to be an official reaction to what they had both witnessed, it would have to come from him. He had noticed during the presentation of the horror show from Mars how Julie's breathing increased. The images—sharp and clear though coming from Mars—were nothing less than overwhelming. "What's the situation now, sir?"

Kelliher smiled. "Secure. So everyone tells me. But I don't believe that. Not after seeing"—he waved his hand at the air as if he could make the creatures that had recently filled the screen disappear—"all that. If Mars City is secure, than so is hell."

Julie leaned forward. "Mr. Kelliher, I see that along with the vids, you have sent us a lot of data."

"Yes."

"The reason?"

Kelliher straightened up in his chair. "I imagine you can guess?"

Julie kept talking—her area of expertise was perhaps the one most relevant here. "Okay, I'm thinking you would like our opinion on the biological makeup, what caused the malformations, the altered behavior?"

David added: "Perhaps guesses as to what biological changes on the nano-level could have transformed people. Is that about it, Mr. Kelliher?"

Kelliher looked away again. And David knew there were secrets that the UAC head was holding close. That whatever was to happen down here, with the data, with the images, they still might not have everything. It might be something for them to question.

"Yes, exactly that. Your ideas, theories, could be important. But there's something else."

David and Julie waited.

Kelliher looked right into the lens. "Your work— it's going well down there?"

Julie jumped right in. "Yes. David sent a report. But in fact today we had an amazing opportunity. A new vent, just opening, and capturing the, well, birth of a new world as it started to happen."

"Good. David? You too—also excited?"

"Yes, absolutely."

"I want—in light of things—to make sure you have the support from me you need. How does that sound?"

Julie nodded. "To be blunt, sir, we almost expected that you were contacting us to give us a shutdown notice."

David watched Kelliher hesitate, and he knew that perhaps—until the events on Mars—that might indeed have been the case. He thought, *We have a new lease on life because of events on Mars, events that not one of the UAC's scientists can explain. Suddenly, what we are doing here is important.*

"I'll be honest too." Kelliher leaned close, as if their completely secure conversation might be overheard. "I'm very concerned. There's too much I don't know. All I know is what I've seen happen up there, this explosion of death, destruction . . ." He licked his lips. "It very much—"

The UAC head sighed, and for the first time since David started working for him, Kelliher looked anything but the all-powerful head of the UAC.

"—scares me."

"We understand, sir."

A rueful smile at the corners of Kelliher's mouth. Again, David felt sure they were not being told everything. "Do you? I'm afraid I don't. Though, trust me, I have every resource of the UAC devoted to examining every single goddamned aspect of what happened up there. But will it be enough? Is there time? Are we smart enough to answer any of those questions?"

"We'll do what we can down here. You can be sure of that," David said. He could feel how empty his words sounded as soon as he uttered them.

"I know. That's why I want you to begin exploring some answers now. What you are doing . . . may take time. And we may never need what you learn. It may just end up being research. Or—well, let's just say I have always played my hunches."

"Yes, sir."

"I want you to use everything you've been finding down there about the alternative ecosystem, the adaptations to extreme heat, the vent creatures' ability to create food from poison, the entire biosystem. And by 'use it,' I don't mean simply understand it. Explain it, then master it. Because I think we—as a species—may need it."

For a moment David didn't have a clue what Kelliher might be referring to. *Need it as a species? What could that mean?*

But Julie, always a step ahead of him, it seemed, did get it.

"Mr. Kelliher, are you suggesting, no . . . *ordering* . . . that we begin immediate work into how the alternate biosystems of the vent life could be studied to see how it might be used to create—"

Kelliher finished her sentence. "Human modifications, yes."

The cloud parted in David's mind, and for a second he felt a chill ripple on his arms. Gooseflesh.

He recovered enough to ask a follow-up question. "Human modifications? Genetic adaptations for human use that would allow people to—" He shook his head, letting the images come. "To resist extremes of cold and heat perhaps. To resist toxins. To be able to even—I don't know—draw sustenance from raw, even deadly chemicals."

Kelliher's answer was as simple as it was chilling. "Yes."

"You are talking about military use of our work down here, is that it?" Julie said.

"Yes, but not to wage wars against other countries—though God knows we will continue to have plenty of them. But what if what happened up there isn't over? Can we really stop them? And are the images, the creatures we've seen—is that all of them? Could this be the last battle, one that will determine whether the species known as human continues? So yes, 'military use,' if you wish to call it that."

Julie looked at David. They both prided themselves on how their underwater kingdom had stayed magically free of the violence and politics of the surface world. Now—no more.

"Right, Mr. Kelliher. I can start redirecting the lab work. The new samples we have, they're already developing. They'll be—"

"Great, David. I've already arranged for teams from around the world to join you down there. I took the liberty of picking some"—a small laugh—"actually *most* of the UAC's best and brightest to get down there immediately. Things may get a bit tight."

David rubbed his chin. "Tight"? That was an understatement. "Yes, sir. We'll start making preparations."

"I will want to be kept posted on any developments, positive or negative."

"Of course."

"But, Julie, David . . . I don't want to micromanage your work. There's really only one thing I want to say."

David saw that Kelliher looked shaken. Did he feel guilty about what had happened on Mars? Was that part of this?

"I can only tell you—instinct again, I guess—that we don't have a lot of time. I have money, resources, the world's finest scientists. But time—who knows how long there may be."

"We'll start immediately."

Kelliher nodded. Then, almost a whisper: "Good luck."

Then the signal vanished.

16

THE THREE MARINES STOOD IN AN L-SHAPED section of sector B of the Alpha Lab complex. Or, as they all had grown to call it, one mighty damn good hiding place. Uri Stavit lit a forbidden cigarette using the burning end of one of his friends' cigarettes, inhaling deeply before turning to one side and hacking into the air.

Of course, smoking anywhere in Mars City was verboten, but with the body cleanup still going on, it was unlikely that anyone would take a big sniff and think, *What the hell is that?* More than enough weird smells all over this place.

One of the other grunts, a guy named Graver, looked at his chronometer. "I say we go for a new record. How long we can hang right here, on this spot, before someone comes looking for us."

The other marine, a guy everyone called "TM," just grinned and sucked on his own smoke.

Uri didn't know them that well, only stealing a smoke from time to time. But he knew that, considering the circumstances, whoever stood next to you was suddenly your new best friend. Their life could be in your hands and, more important, vice versa.

"What do you think, Uri? We just hang here?" Graver wore a big smile. "A little hide-and-seek from the brass?" He slapped his head in mock horror. "Oh, we don't have any brass running our part of this circus, do we? And who made Moraetes queen? Does she even outrank us?"

"I think," Uri said, "she has a few stripes. She'd been here awhile. But then she had that incident."

The other two nodded. Everyone knew about Moraetes. It was the stuff of legend: a private saves some VIP's ass, not even just any VIP, but Kelliher, the head of the UAC—and she gets on Hayden's shit-list, maybe forever.

Of course, Kelliher did catch a bullet. But he was still alive, he was fucking breathing. All due to her. Uri didn't say it, but if came to taking orders from Moraetes, he had no doubt where he stood.

As for the other two clowns? They could make all the jokes they wanted to, but he guessed that they too would do exactly what Moraetes asked.

TM looked at the last centimeter or so of his home-rolled butt. "You know, next time, I suggest we spice up the tobacco a bit."

Graver nodded and smiled. "Amen, brother. I know a dude who can get us some—"

Uri nodded in agreement, though he doubted he'd want to be hiding in these dark corridors, getting high. That experience he could do without—it could all wait until he was back in Tel Aviv, on the beach, a perfect sunny day, maybe with some beautiful girl with him, worlds away from this insanity. Yeah, that would be the place to get stoned.

He took another drag of the cigarette, already feeling the bitter taste on his tongue. Sucking in the smoke, then one final puff. He ended with a big cough—it wasn't like he smoked every day.

Graver opened his mouth, turning to TM. Another burst of bullshit about to be launched, Uri guessed. But amazingly, he couldn't hear a thing. After the gulp of smoke, the cough, the desire for air, Uri felt the urgent rush to reward the lungs with what they really needed. But there was nothing.

Graver's mouth was open, but then he seemed to realize that something was wrong somewhere. TM's face—in those tiny seconds of clarity—registered *what?*

They should have been prepared, Uri thought. After everything they had seen today. But maybe humans are wired to assume that, yeah, it's okay now. Everything's cool. Problem solved, monsters gone, all the dying done for today. Maybe that's how we get through things. That little trick, the delusion.

Then suddenly, like someone yanking on a leash to snap some stupid dog back into place, that terrible, horrible tug of reality. The pain overwhelming. Quick calculations—and Uri stepped back from where the two corridors intersected. Something had sucked the air out of the corridor, and now it rushed back, a tsunami of air, blowing Graver's hair, making TM's face ripple.

Uri could hear their yells, the screams, the few barked words of confusion, trying to marshal each other's brain to understand and—Christ—do *something*.

But with the air came the noise, and having seen what happened last time, Uri pressed tight against the wall, neatly into a corner, and waited for the inevitable, waited for what came next.

In Delta Lab, Dr. Kellyn MacDonald tasted something on his lips. His tongue was dry, a cracked leathery thing, but it could still move. The stuff on his lips moist, sticky. *Blood?* he thought. *My blood? Someone else's? Or something else, some new substance from, from—*

The Other Place.

That's what he called it, the place where all these things came from. The parade of creatures emerged from the teleportation pod that Kellyn could see— oh so clearly now—was a portal.

Yes, a portal. A door. And doors led somewhere, right? So what was this place? Where—for the love of God, if there was a God anymore—did the portal go? He brought a hand to his cheek and rubbed the stuff off his lips. There, gone. He had long ago passed being desperately thirsty. Now he had only one message he kept repeating to his brain: *If you stay still, if you don't move, you maybe*—maybe—*can still live*.

Though he was smart enough to know now that *that* was highly unlikely. Improbable, as they say.

He had hoped to get another message to Kelliher, telling him the answers were all in his previous encoded messages. That there was an explanation there. Now MacDonald imagined that there would be no more messages out. And his family? They would have seen by now his last transmission, his sad words of love, how he had done all this for them. Telling them how he had believed in the importance of it all, how it could have built their future. From Earth to Mars, a future together that he knew now was gone forever.

He could so easily start crying again, but a small part of his brain overruled that indulgence. After all, he knew that just past this small alcove, the lab was now filled. The parade of creatures building, the room hitting capacity, ladies and gentlemen.

Delta had been locked down, sealed off. Did anyone on the outside have a clue what was happening here? Were there still any a/v feeds out? He doubted that. The place was sealed tight as more and more things . . . just poured into it.

He wanted to cover his ears because, even though the killing in here seemed to have stopped, even though there were no more human screams begging release from whatever horror preyed on them, he could still somehow hear them. Hear the sounds, the grunts, the muffled roaring and guttural sounds. An unearthly horror that, well, had anyone ever heard before? Outside of a madhouse, that is.

Then, so quickly, everything changed. He saw the room glow as if a lurid orange-red beacon had been turned on, an alternate sun now streaming into the room, blinding in its bloodred light.

The chattering and garbled roars began to assume a rhythmic quality. Were they trying to talk? God, were these things trying to communicate? And what triggered the sounds?

MacDonald knew he should stay there, curled up like one of the yet unrevived corpses. But how could he? If any role was assigned to him, it was that of observer, someone to record what happened here. Would that save others? Could others even be saved?

He didn't torture his mind with those questions.

Slowly his shaking hands locked on the edge of this lab table, off in a dark corner, shielding him from the red sunlike glow that filled the room. He started even more slowly to bring his head up, knowing that his skull would emerge before his eyes could see . . .

Until he had his eyes at the table edge, squinting at that brilliant sick glow, and he could see everything that happened next.

17

I HAVE A NAME, HE THOUGHT. EVEN AS A ROAR-ing train of sound and light rocketed past him, almost ripping him away from his crouching position at the wall, he kept thinking, *I have a name. I'm, I'm—*

And he knew that if he couldn't recall his name now, and who he was, that something would begin to slip, that whatever still roared past him would somehow be able to touch him, capture him—

Change him.

So he absolutely knew he had to fight to keep coming back to that point. *My name,* my life—I had it just a few seconds ago. It's just there, sweet God, it was just there. Please don't let it just vanish.

And for a moment he thought it was hopeless, that there was no way he could recover such information, now lost, so distant, perhaps unimportant in whatever new way of life was about to begin.

But then the roaring noise seemed to ebb, and with it, the light, the color, began to fade. The roaring express moved on, seeing other corners, other people. And then—there it was:

I'm Uri. And I'm okay.

The thought was enough to make him giddy, the realization that somehow he had survived, that he had resisted whatever force had been in the corridor with him. Was he spared because he had plastered himself into a corner, the angle of the reinforced metal walls protecting him? Was that why he was untouched?

Like any survivor, for those few seconds he stood in that magical moment when you realize you've been given a great and wondrous gift. Yet for any survivor, those seconds are just that, so brief, as reality and its demands come roaring back. Only in this case, the reality that Uri faced probably deserved another name.

Because he stood facing Graver and TM. At least, he imagined that's who they were . . . or what they were. The upper part of their uniforms hung off them in shreds. Both had open gashes, and while there was something seeping and gleaming in those long open wounds, it wasn't blood.

His two fellow marines had something else under their skin. Questions flew into his mind quickly. How could that happen so . . . *fast?* Their blood transformed or replaced. And the ultimate survivor's question: why them, and not me?

Only seconds, and then they both turned to him. Their faces barely recognizable. Twisted and broken masks of what used to be the way they looked. TM's jaw hung open as if broken and detached. But a sudden quick snap, as if he were trying it out, showed Uri that this new configuration worked just fine.

Graver's arm, twisted and corkscrewed around, still held a gun. While the muscle and tissue connecting the upper arm to the lower looked like it could break apart, that too also worked well as Graver started raising the weapon at the same moment as his tongue snaked out, tasting the air.

They weren't human anymore.

Uri raised his own weapon. Shooting them was not going to be hard at all. But while he took aim at Graver, whose muzzle now was leveled at Uri, TM reached out and grabbed at Uri's shoulder, the move quick and unexpected.

TM's hand began to close on the indentation of Uri's right shoulder. The pain was overwhelming, blinding. Uri knew that if he let it get to him, then his brief moment as survivor would be over. And in fact, his fate—since he was fully conscious—could be worse than theirs.

He fired at Graver, their guns only a meter apart, and as he did, he ducked to his left. He felt a chunk of his flesh being ripped off in that move as the TM thing held tight.

And his shot didn't seem to stop Graver, who merely pivoted and started spraying the wall with bullets. But as Uri fell back, he realized something: that whatever his buddies had become, whatever shreds of weapons knowledge still resided inside their misshapen heads, it wasn't the full deal.

Maybe they were taking directions from somewhere else. Human instinct—the basic reflexes drilled into them in Quantico practicing close-quarters firefights—had vanished. Sure, they could move, and grab and pull triggers and even have some kind of goddamn aim.

But Uri was still human. And amazingly, that still counted for something.

Rolling onto his back, completely vulnerable, he raised his weapon and fired à circular burst into TM's head. The shots proved effective, as TM stopped moving and then fell to his knees as if being called to prayer.

A quick few inches over, and another blast at Graver, a bit off the mark this time, but the first round pushed the zombie marine back until Uri could use the thing's head for target practice.

And that's exactly how he thought about it. Just another target, real close, and—

Don't even think that if you screw up, your life is gone.

Graver dropped his weapon, then its two hands—and Uri could see that they no longer looked like hands—went to the bullet-riddled face as if it could pick out the bullets, like removing a dust speck from an eye.

Until Graver too fell to his knees, and then fell forward, right at Uri's feet.

Then, for the second time, Uri had the same feeling as before. With his heart still racing, chugging his breaths in and out as though gasping for his last breath, he had the feeling: *I'm alive.*

And having had that miraculous feeling twice now, he told himself, *I'm going to keep it that way.*

But that would require allies. So he scrambled to his feet and started to plan where he had to go and how to get there without losing his life.

Dr. Kellyn MacDonald stared at the edge of the metal lab table. He made sure not to move his head. He sat in the shadows here, but even the slightest movement might get their attention. So he had to hold his head perfectly steady and let his eyes scan the room, taking in everything that he could see that way, and thinking—

Make no sound. I must not make . . . a . . . sound.

His eyes swung back and forth. For some of the things that filled the lab, he could only make out shapes. Some of them had once been his peers, the other scientists, now only recognizable because of their white lab coats. Other things lumbered near them, pushing them aside, moving to the opening that led out of Delta.

And MacDonald thought: *It's open, the lab is open again!*

His eyes swiveled back to take in more of the creatures, the things that had emerged from the pod . . . the portal. He focused on one that—at first—he thought was a group of spindly-legged things walking together. Until, even in the smoky shadows of the lab, he could see it was clearly one creature.

One creature. And those spindly things, the legs, how many of them were there? He tried counting . . . one, two, three, four . . . but it moved, and he started over, as if getting the number of legs right was somehow important.

But then he got distracted by what sat atop the spiderlike creature—which was the only thing Mac-Donald could compare it to, with all those legs moving together, carrying the creature forward.

Something sat on top of it, he saw. But no, nothing *rode* this thing. What he took for another creature was part of it, attached to it. And just then he watched the spiderlike creature's head turn, as if it sensed something scrutinizing it.

MacDonald dared not move. But he could close his eyes, cutting off the possibility of any reflective glare from the pools of milky white sclera and the dark horrified pupil at each eye's center.

And in that moment the thing might have spotted him, stopped, and used those spindly legs (which MacDonald imagined *surely* must have the spiky hairs he had seen only under a microscope, but now each inches long, leathery and sharp) to scramble over toward him.

He waited, holding his breath. Then, as if the action could make any noise at all, he slowly opened his eyes.

It had moved on, followed by others. MacDonald let his eyes slowly move right, back to the portal that had allowed these beings in.

When he did, he saw another shape coming out, indistinct at first, but slowly resolving itself into something—at first—reassuringly human.

Dr. Betruger. Only now Betruger no longer held the artifact U1—the so-called Soul Cube. It was gone, having been carried by him into wherever the portal led.

And MacDonald felt a hopelessness that made the very thought of escape, of the future, of planning, as absurd as the death struggle of an ant with its legs removed, fighting somehow, for some reason . . . to stay alive.

18

KANE STARED AT THE IMPLODED DOOR OF THE elevator shaft. He tapped his earpiece, but there was still no signal. He had heard the roaring sound of a new blast racing through Mars City, and had pressed himself into an alcove, hoping it would miss him.

Apparently this one not only took out communications, but it also caused new structural damage that was going to make getting to Alpha hard.

He had hoped he could reach Maria and confirm she was okay. And he wondered: *Back at Reception— what had happened there?* Once again, he was alone, no way to contact anyone, and with an increasingly twisted maze of metal seemingly working against him all the way.

Alone.

Guess I better get used to it, he realized. Down on Earth he had always felt alone except maybe for those times he could share a decent bourbon with Master Sergeant Chadbourne. But watching his sergeant die in Terekstan, turned into a red cloud, just reminded Kane that you don't connect to anyone. Not in this job.

Is that what this was, a job? Some people sit at desks. Some work in labs. Some try to squeeze more food out of an ever-reluctant planet Earth. And what was his job? Kill or be killed? Use every bit of firepower that the government gives him to destroy things?

He pulled up his PDA. It had been good thinking, making the core information system independent of any functioning network. In seconds, he was scrolling through the different ways to Alpha. He saw the nearby elevator shaft on the map, now useless.

And then he saw the nearby emergency stairs leading to transport tunnels that went almost straight all the way through to Alpha before arriving at another row of supply elevators. Would they be functional? And what was waiting for him downstairs?

If anyone was running this show, they'd probably order him back to Reception to fortify the position there. They'd want anyone who survived to regroup. But there was no brass telling him anything. And he had obviously shown he wasn't too good at taking orders anyway.

So it would be the stairs, and run to Alpha.

No, he admitted. *To Maria.* After all, you've got to care about something in this "job."

Otherwise it's just bullets and blood.

Kane started for the closest stairway down.

Theo didn't move a muscle. *They* were down there. He could hear them, taking steps, like they might move away.

But they just stood, waiting, like they were playing a game of hide-and-seek. And soon he'd make a sound, and they'd know where he was, and they—they—

What would they do? He had tried so hard not to imagine it. But he could keep the thoughts away for only so long. Just like when he'd be in his bed at night, in the dark, and the things from his dreams would seem to be there, in his room, hiding, and he would force his voice to call out for his mother, so afraid that the call would make them leap out. Land on him. Grab him. Bite down. . . .

He could see them with only one eye through the tiny crack in the airshaft that went across this corridor. They didn't talk or make any sounds. And these weren't soldiers. No, they wore pieces of what looked like white shirts—like those his dad wore—hanging off them.

One looked as though it held something shiny, metallic, in its hand. Scissors. But then the longer he stared at that arm with his one eye, the more he could see that the thing wasn't *holding* the scissors. No, the scissors were part of the thing's arm. A hand, or what used to be a hand, now attached to the scissors.

Theo looked away.

He felt something in his nose. A bit of dust. *No*, he thought. *I can't sneeze. Please, don't make me sneeze.* But he could feel his nostrils tingling, and the more he thought about *not* sneezing, the more it seemed that it had to happen. In only seconds, he'd sneeze—

And they'd know he was there.

He brought a hand up to his nose, moving it slowly because even that movement could be heard. He rubbed his nose, trying to make the sneeze not happen. Even as he did that, he felt that sudden intake of air. A burp of air, and then the explosion out.

As soon as he sneezed, he looked through the crack, but the two things below him were gone. Had they moved away in that instant?

But no, that would have been too lucky. And behind him, a few feet away, he saw something cut up and into the shaft. The scissors! Like a giant crab claw, cutting into the metal so easily,

He looked away, ready to start crawling down the shaft as fast as he could in the other direction when he saw two clawlike hands jab through the metal like it was only cardboard, holding on to the ragged edges.

And he was in the middle as one thing ripped at the metal ahead, while the other pulled out its scissors hands and started jabbing into the shaft, closer and closer to Theo.

Uri trotted back toward Delta and what he hoped would be a sizeable force with Sergeant Kelly. Somehow he had just found the adrenaline to take out what used to be two of his buddies. But he guessed the odds down here for a lone human weren't going to go from bad to worse.

He heard sounds as he jogged down the long, seemingly empty shaft. More sounds than just his boots slapping down on the metal floor. Weird howls, moans, and grunts that came from animals that we certainly didn't have on Earth. That is, unless they were sounds that humans could make.

When humans were pushed to a strange new limit of madness and pain, was that the kind of sounds they made?

But the corridor ahead remained eerily empty.

He had been glad to get away from Delta when Kelly assigned the three of them to patrol down here. Now the only thing he could think of was to get back there. Such a human instinct, he realized. Get with more of the species. Maybe one of them will get picked off instead of you. Get near the center of the pack, and let one of *them* get taken.

He held his machine gun in the raised and ready position. If anything got in his way, he'd shoot first and wonder what the hell it was later. No time for peering into the shadows. Just spray whatever moved with bullets, that was the plan. Got plenty of ammo. Just shoot and shoot and—

He stopped.

Ahead, a door. Nothing too dramatic about that. There were a few airlock doors between here and Kelly's position outside Delta. No big problem, right?

Except . . . Uri licked his lips, hating a terrible fact that he couldn't avoid, a fact that came popping into his head, unwanted, persistent . . . and ultimately undeniable.

That door had been open. So someone—or something—had shut the door.

His hand flexed a bit around the trigger of the gun. Had the blast that rocketed through Mars City made the door shut? Could that have done it? Was that the reason the door was now shut?

A sudden howl erupted from behind him. More of those high-pitched, guttural squeals.

He realized two things: that he didn't know what shut that door.

And that he had no choice, none at all, but to walk up to it, open it, and keep going. The horrific sounds behind him reminded him of that.

19

KANE CLIMBED OVER TO A PAIR OF TWISTED metal girders that had fallen into each other, making a perfect X, blocking the way forward. The destruction down here varied wildly, with some sections intact and others looking as though a massive detonation had ripped the place apart.

What determined whether one spot got hit and another spared? He didn't know, but Kane imagined it had something to with why certain people were transformed by whatever emanated from Delta, and others could avoid it. It all depended on how the red tide of light and color hit you, or even if it hit you at all.

His right knee sent a spike to his brain, reminding him that he still had a dozen parts of his body that could all use medical attention. He had injected a stim just after the first outbreak, but already he felt it wearing off. There was a limited time he could continue using them before his body would fail to respond even to the injection of chemicals telling him that, somehow, he could keep going.

He had—he guessed—at best two hours before he'd collapse. *Not a lot of time. . . .*

He crawled his way through the maze of metal and stood up. No lights ahead. Even the emergency lighting system throughout the complex had gone spotty and erratic. And ahead of that loomed nothing but blackness. He grabbed his small tungsten flashlight from his side. Not designed for navigating dark subterranean corridors, the small flashlight was for doing close-up work where you needed more light.

He turned it on. The light, bright and piercing, still shed only a small pool. And when Kane pointed it dead ahead, that milky-white pool faded into the gloom.

But it was all he had.

He looked at his gun, the magazine now full with the ammo he had found on a pair of dead marines he passed. There was another magazine strapped to his left side. His pistol was also fully loaded, with plenty of ammo rounds left for that. He was as set as he was going to be.

He started walking down the hallway.

Campbell lifted up the metal case slowly. The metal hinges made a creak that filled this secure room off the transport area. The transport area had been deserted—everyone scrambling to get someplace safe, or trying to join their squad.

Nobody wanted to be stuck out here alone. He couldn't blame them.

The case lid up, Campbell looked look down at the

gun. It had been his idea to bring it up. No telling what could happen, he had told Kelliher. They had one version of the situation from Hayden, another from Betruger, and still a third in the disturbing images from Kelliher's mole, Dr. Kellyn MacDonald.

"I'd like to bring up a BFG-9000," he had told Kelliher. "Just in case." And there was no argument. Now Campbell slid one hand under the massive stock of the gun and another under the thick barrel, which was surrounded by a hydraulic cooling system. The gun wouldn't do much good if it overheated. And with the ability to reload in seconds, this massive weapon was made for long-term, nonstop shooting of its heavy-duty shells.

And now Campbell knew that there would be plenty of things to shoot.

He lifted the gun out and slid its reinforced strap over his shoulder. For such a big gun, the weight wasn't too much of a killer. The newest polycarbonate and synthetic metals made it as light as it could be, and the design—for something that looked so awkward—was also incredibly well balanced.

The BFG. It was, in fact, *the* Biggest Fucking Gun. Unless the desert labs of the New World Terrorist Confederation were working on something bigger, something to take into the streets of New York or Moscow. Campbell doubted it.

He touched a button, and the gun's computer-assisted targeting system came on. The targeting system immediately linked to an infrared HUD. But for now Campbell would just use his eyes. If he hit spots where the emergency lighting was out, the gun had its own mounted lights.

And though it was more than well suited to annihilating whatever creatures Delta Lab seemed to be spawning, there was something else he might have to use it for.

Swann was still out there. Cut off from any contact with Mars City Command. And that had Campbell worried. What if Swann made a decision on his own—a bad decision? What if Swann began to think that getting the Comm Center up and contacting the Armada was a good idea? What if he got through, and before anyone could stop it, the Armada came here, landed troops, brought the big transports down? What would happen then?

If there was one thing Campbell knew, it was this: whatever was happening here on Mars had to stay here. Even if it meant that every still-human soul on the Red Planet died.

Whatever happened here couldn't get back to Earth.

He gave the big gun a slight shake. The small control board on the weapon showed that all its high-tech systems were ready, ammo fully engaged, targeting assistance available.

It was a long way to the Comm Center. And only God knew what he'd find along the way.

Or maybe, he thought, *even God doesn't know anymore.*

There was no time to waste, so he stepped out of the storage room and started heading into the mayhem that filled the halls and corridors and labs of Mars City.

Slash!

The open mouth of the scissor blades, twisting on the end of an arm, hacked at the metal, chewing their way to Theo.

The boy kept whipping his head from front to back, turning away from the scissors to the hands that had somehow smashed into the shaft.

He started sucking air in and out fast as he realized that he was trapped. Every second brought them closer to him, and there was no way that he could get past them. He wanted to close his eyes so badly. Just close them, and this would all go away. But he knew that wouldn't make these monsters disappear. In fact, he knew that would only mean he wouldn't see which one of them got him.

And what would they do when they got hold of him?

Would they fight over him, like dogs back on Earth tugging at the same bone dug out of a garbage can, snarling and pulling at it?

No, he told himself. *Don't think about that.* There was only one thing he should think about: how to escape. Maybe he could find his father in the lab.

Though he didn't really think his dad was okay. Not anymore. . . .

He kept looking to see if there was any way past the two things ripping the metal to get at him. There had to be a way, had to be—

But he could see that there wasn't. *No way to escape.*

Suddenly Theo felt himself move. The section of the shaft started falling. He felt that same giddy feeling in his stomach that he did on the rides in the amusement park that opened each summer.

Back on Earth, back when he was safe . . .

Now the chunk of shaft tumbled forward. Theo pasted his hands against the metal sides even as he felt the shaft smash to the floor and roll over, once, then again—the piece turning into some fun-house ride.

But when it stopped, he saw two open ends.

Open, with no grabbing hands there, no scissors slicing at the metal.

And with every moment he spent in this world, Theo was learning things. Learning how to stay alive.

Like how important it was to be fast. To move fast, act fast. To move without thinking.

He picked one of the shaft openings and, ignoring the jagged bits of metal that sliced and caught at his clothing and skin, he scurried out, not letting himself think about what would happen next.

20

MARIA LOOKED AROUND THE JUNCTION OF THE two corridors, one leading back to Reception, the other to Alpha. At her feet lay marines who only minutes ago had been talking to her, counting their good fortune that—hell, yeah—they were alive.

Now they were all dead, still oozing what was once blood but somehow had changed so quickly into something thicker, darker. The bodies, riddled with bullets, gave off a stench and thin funnels of steam as if the shots had opened fissures to something deep and subterranean.

I've seen a lot of things, Maria thought. *But this . . . this—*

Her stomach tightened, and she felt that wave—again—of revulsion and fear, a feeling that she couldn't continue, that maybe she best give up. She tapped her earpiece, then looked over at Andy Kim, standing a few feet away, his gun also still pointed at the pile of corpses.

"Andy, you okay?" Andy nodded, but his glassy eyes remained fixed on the bodies. "Andy! You okay?" She had raised her voice, and now the other private turned to her.

"Yeah. Just great, Maria. Couldn't be better."

Maria smiled at him. "Me too."

Thinking: *Come on, Andy. Smile back. Break the tension. 'Cause if I'm here all alone, I'm not sure I can hold it together.* Finally Andy allowed a half smile to make his lips turn up at the side.

Good, she thought. *The more we can act like goddamn human beings, the better.*

"Anything on your earpiece?" she asked. She knew the answer to that. Of course there was nothing. The system was maybe down for the count this time. Just an expression for most people, but Maria, with her thirty-three professional bouts, knew what that meant. When an opponent hit the mat and the referee started counting . . . and you stood there, if you were the person who decked the other boxer, and hoped that the person wouldn't get up.

Because she knew too well how quickly the tide could turn. If they got up, driven by hunger or desire or some crazed burst of adrenaline, anything could happen, and the whole story could change.

Are we down for the count, too? she wondered. *What's happening throughout the Mars complex? How many left alive? How many of these things walking around? Is help coming, and will it be enough help?*

"Maria," Andy said, "what the hell are we going to do?"

"Good question." She looked up and down the

corridors. On her orders, two patrols had set off, one to Alpha, the other back to Reception. Without a radio, she couldn't tell what was going on. Were they dead, transformed, or even now hurrying back here?

"I think—" She looked at her watch, wondering how much time had gone by since she sent them out. Was it twenty minutes ago? Thirty? They could be heading here. "Okay, I think we should stay right here for a—"

"You're kidding me. Here? And wait for more of them to come?"

"Look. Either way we got a clean shot at anything that comes to this point. If it looks like it isn't a human . . . anymore, we can blow it away. I think we need to see if any of the others make it back, then plan where we go—together. Could be the radio will come back on by then."

"I doubt that."

"Lot of things to doubt, Andy. Including my ideas. But I think to move now, without knowing anything, without waiting to see what happened to the others—that's crazy."

Andy looked away from her, back to the pile. He said his next words with eyes locked on the pile of bodies. "How long? How long . . . do we stay here?"

"Let's give it fifteen. If no one returns in that time, we move to Plan B."

"And that is?"

"We go to one of two places. To Delta. Kelly was

there. Lot of marines with him. Can't all be dead or—you know."

"I know. What's the other place?"

"We go to Reception. That way transport is close, and if somebody got the word out to the Armada, they could be close already. More marines, and an old-fashioned rescue."

"*If* they got word out." Now he looked back up. "*If* they were willing to come down here." He raised his voice, and the sound of it frightened Maria.

Come on, Andy. Hold it together.

"If they didn't think that whatever's happening here is too dangerous."

Maria took a breath through her mouth. The stench seemed to grow the longer the bodies sat there. "You asked for a Plan B. There, you got it. Plan B." Now she looked at her watch for real. "I said fifteen minutes. So now, look alive, gun ready, and we wait."

They both glanced to the two long dark shafts, lit only by the emergency lighting that was glaringly bright in spots, and barely reached the outer areas.

Andy clicked the ammo chamber of his gun, moving the clip out of, then into, position.

"All set. Start the clock."

"Started."

Kane's small flashlight flickered. *Come on*, he thought. *Don't die. Don't tell me they issued me one of these little flashlights with a low charge.*

He tapped it and made the light bounce back to

life. And even though the small circle of light shooting through the gloom seemed pretty pathetic, Kane was glad for it.

He walked slowly, making sure he didn't outpace the ability of the light to show what was ahead. Wouldn't do to walk into something hugging a wall and have it reach out and grab him.

I've been damn lucky so far, Kane thought. *Beat up a bit. But alive.* Luck could change, and he also knew there was a limit to what the stim injections could do. Fatigue must eventually take over, and his judgment would slip, his reflexes would fail, his muscles would begin to lose their trained ability to respond.

So how much time did he have? Kane wasn't sure he wanted to know.

He came to an L in the corridor—always a tricky moment when you can't see what's on the other side. All he could do was move as far to the right as possible. He slowed his pace even more. And with every step, he listened. Was there something there, waiting?

Back on Earth he had access to all sorts of devices that could let him see around a corner like this. Even something as simple as one of those old recon scopes—heck, even a mirror would do the trick. But now, here, he had nothing.

Another step. All quiet. He took a breath, half prepared for something to leap out as soon as his head cleared the corner. The muzzle of his gun remained level with his head.

As soon as he could see around the L, he could shoot there. As if that might make a difference. . . .

One last step—and Kane had to wonder why he felt so cautious here. The fatigue? Instinct? Was all this insanity finally getting to him?

And then he was at the point where he could see into the other corridor, and now his light immediately grew even more pathetic. This section of the corridor opened up to twice the height, and much wider, though a quick scan with the flashlight showed a series of large curved areas.

He stopped and pulled up the PDA, quickly making the map of this section come to life. *Hydrocon Reservoirs.* The Hydrocons were essential to Mars City, providing clean hydrogen fuel, with pure water as a by-product. It was technology ultimately intended for Earth, but would it ever get there? The units here worked well enough, according to the PR info on his PDA, but they were still in prototype stages.

Kane didn't think that Earth had time to wait for any prototyping. If they work, start building them.

He started down the corridor, walking right in the middle, moving his flashlight from left to right. The Hydrocon Reservoirs hid dark recesses where anything was possible. The other wall bore the signs of the stress and explosions from above, dimpled here and there as though someone had backed an armored ARV into it.

Nobody else down here.

And Kane thought—not for the first time—how

great it would be to have Chadbourne with him, cutting the tension with some crack that somehow made it seem like the two of them could face anything. Or Tompkins, absolutely fearless because he had seen far worse in the streets of what they now called Outer New York.

Yeah, Earth needed the Hydrocon technology fast. And anything else they might learn on Mars.

Well, not exactly. They didn't need whatever roared through the complex and transformed humans into zombies. Or made other things appear from who knew where, those tall monsters (*Such a stupid word*, he thought again), and that dog thing he had killed back near Reception. No, Earth didn't need those.

He swung the light left, a steady rhythm back and forth, scanning each side, his gun muzzle following the light. And he didn't change that pattern until he heard a sound from above, and only then brought the light slowly up to the tall ceiling.

But what he saw moved so fast that the light really didn't do much good at all.

21

INSTANTLY, ALL SIGNALS FROM MARS CITY were simply gone. Ian Kelliher tried hitting some of the keys on the floating screen before him, hoping against hope that it was some local problem, maybe only his own feed somehow malfunctioning. But his instincts were too well trained to allow that faint flicker of a possibility more than a moment's existence.

Something had happened again on Mars. Immediately an analogy popped into Kelliher's head: it was like when you feel an earthquake tremor, and then it all goes quiet while everyone braces for what will surely be the real thing, the big one to come.

He had hoped that Hayden was right, that everything was secure, Delta all locked down, the situation slowly getting back under control.

(And all the monsters were dead. No more monsters now, folks, and we can all go back to business as usual.)

"Fat fucking chance," Kelliher whispered, repeating one of his father's favorite expressions. His father was never one to leave anything to chance. Chance is for fools, Tommy Kelliher used to tell him. Once you're waiting for chance to give you a break, you might as well put a gun to your head because you've lost control.

Had Kelliher done just that? He had let himself believe—hope—that all was well. And now, with this, he could barely imagine what was happening. The images from the first outbreak were sufficient fodder to feed a thousand nightmare scenarios.

"Karla, can you check with Captain Hakala on the *Missouri?* See if he's getting anything from Mars."

"Yes, Mr. Kelliher."

Hakala was actually a man that Kelliher was considering to take over Mars City. Hayden was always too much under Betruger's wing. He never knew what to believe—or not—whenever Hayden spoke. Hakala would be a completely different commander running the base.

Of course, if that meant the Armada came to the rescue, the UAC might have no say in the matter anyway.

He had even launched his request to the Pentagon, who technically still controlled both Hayden and Hakala, no matter how much they were in bed with the UAC. But the Pentagon wanted to keep Hakala exactly where he was. It might all be a moot point soon . . .

And again Kelliher wondered: Should he have simply sent the Armada directly to Mars, not merely standing by? Could what had just happened have been prevented in any way? If he had ordered Hayden to do just that, then the Armada would have landed—a thousand space marines strong, two large research and support ships, and the first true planetary battle cruiser.

And why did we need a battle cruiser in our star system? people may have wondered. But Kelliher and the close circle of generals that he briefed had been able—so far—to dodge that question.

"Sir, I just heard back from Captain Hakala's comm chief. No signals whatsoever emanating from anywhere on the planet."

"Christ . . ." Kelliher said.

"And, sir, they also said that includes the planetary sensors, which have absolutely nothing to do with the main Mars City CommLink or—for that matter—the old Comm Center, which is still technically viable."

"Thanks, Karla. If you get any more info—direct to me. Okay?"

"Yes, sir."

Kelliher sat there. There was nothing he could do now. Nothing but wait until the signal came back. *If* it came back.

He put his hand on his chin and rubbed. And for the first time in a very long time he began to wonder if what was happening was anything at all that he could deal with.

BALLARD RESEARCH STATION
THE MID-ATLANTIC RIDGE

"What do you think?" Julie stood behind David as he looked at the samples "live."

"God, I don't know. But you say"—he turned to look at her—"that it happens this way each time?"

"Yes. I mean, we never got samples at such an early stage, so it's like looking into the beginning of time. If we couldn't hold them in stasis, in a few hours it would be all over. As it is—"

"You get to see every step?"

She took a breath and blew a few stray strands of hair off her forehead. "*Almost* every step, We still don't know if there's anything missing in the progression from inert matter to what becomes the bacteria that feeds off the toxic material. Something clicks, and suddenly what was simply a string of rather strange amino acids and proteinlike material is suddenly 'alive.' That is, if you call this alive."

"Looks like it to me."

For a second David permitted himself to just look at Julie. When they had been together, it had never been smooth. Arguments over procedures and science mixed in with their massive fears of commitment and change. In the end it proved a lethal cocktail to their relationship, which ended politely. Now, looking at her, working with her on something that both of them knew could be so incredibly important, all those differences didn't seem to matter much. He wondered: Did she feel the same way?

The few moments' reverie over, he looked away with his next question. "What about the next step?"

"That's the tricky one. If this is going to have any relevance to life on surface Earth, we have to see what really happens when the bacteria begins establishing connections to potential organic material."

"Right. Is that material already ticking toward true life, or does the bacteria somehow trigger it . . . ?"

"Exactly."

"And out of my field, I'm afraid. But I would like to see whenever you have something, no matter the time of day, or night . . ." A small grin. "Whatever, whenever."

"Oh, you will. I have my team on sixteen-hour shifts. Some sleep, some quick intake of food, then they're back at it. When I see something, I will show you. When do Kelliher's people arrive?"

Kelliher's people. Some of his key scientific team. Resources were being made available also, including two new submersibles on their way, a state-of-the-art data system that—up to now—was only for joint UAC-US projects. All that had changed. Suddenly, their work miles below the surface had become important. *If you live long enough, anything can happen.*

"Their transport chopper is due above our position just after noon. It will take them a while to organize how to ferry everything down. I expect you'll be able to give your new charges their marching orders by 1800 hours."

"Whoa! Marching orders?" Julie said. "I'm going to be running them?"

"Who else? Hopefully they'll be quick learners."

"Do you know their credentials? I get the feeling that I probably should be working under them."

Another smile. "Maybe. Me too perhaps. But for now you're in charge, I run interference and planning, and you just got a team of award-winning scientists to call your own."

Then a smile back from Julie. "Guess I better produce results, hm?"

"That would be my suggestion."

"Okay, then. Get out of here, and let me get back to work."

David sat up. For a moment he wanted to give her a hug. It just seemed like such a natural impulse. "Good luck, Julie. And let me know . . . when there's something to know."

She nodded. Did she sense his impulse too? Or

was he just lost in the ever-painful memories of what used to be—and what couldn't be again?

He turned and walked out of the lab, back to the control room, monitoring the approach of Kelliher's reinforcements racing to them . . . while Mars and its problems couldn't have seemed farther away.

22

KANE'S SMALL LIGHT COULDN'T CATCH whatever was moving around him. But instinctively he threw himself close to a wall. He heard something land on the floor, then another sound. Things falling from above, all around him.

He swung the light to cut a circle around his feet, and that's when he saw his first one. It looked like a spider, only with a body the size of a dog, supported by spindly legs that had the angularity of metal struts. Hell, they might actually have been metal struts.

The light made the one in the glare pull back a bit, but only for a second. In moments it scurried right back toward Kane. And even as Kane blasted, he kept his light on that one. He knew there were others, but he hoped he could use that recoil response, especially if he stayed in the shadows and the spider-thing in the light.

His rounds flicked off a few legs. Kane got a better look at the body, seeing something on top of it that looked like another small creature riding it, rearing back and forth, a mouth open, in fact opening so wide it seemed larger than the head itself. He fired another blast right at whatever protruded on top, and the thing stopped.

Not missing a beat—but noticing how he kept sucking air in and out so fast—he raised the light to see the room *alive* with the things. He swung the small torch back and forth. The startled things skittered a bit, but not nearly with the reaction he noticed with the first one.

Then he saw all of them move straight to him. There was no way even his best shooting could stop them all. Kane took a marine's last resort when all options were gone.

He retreated.

In this case, Kane began running along the wall as he shut the light off. Perhaps they were now using it to mark his position. Either way, with their eyes now used to the light, best to throw them back in the dark.

Kane rested his hand along the wall to guide himself back to where the Hydrocon containers began. But even as he ran in that direction, he knew that he'd soon reach a place with some emergency light where they could actually see him backlit.

And then it would be a one-man Custer's Last Stand. All those tiny legs leaping on him, grabbing and holding on. Then those too-wide mouths. Could be the spider-things had a lot of growing to do.

So Kane stopped, and without turning on his small light, he set down a steady spray of fire in the direction of the creatures. He performed two full sweeps, then clicked the light on again. Nothing. He turned the flashlight so the lamp faced into the corridor and then banged the butt end against the metal wall of the corridor. The damn light came on.

Some things never change, he thought.

And he turned in the direction of the spiders. But one had already leaped up high onto his thigh, the viselike grip of its legs excruciating as they closed with such amazing power for something so small. Now Kane had to point the gun straight down and hope he'd hit the thing and miss his leg . . . or his foot.

A total crapshoot, with no time for anything resembling careful aiming. He blasted away, hitting the creature's midsection, and it exploded like a piñata, the body popping, spraying Kane, the spider legs flying off him—save one, which seemed in a permanently locked position.

With no time to deal with that, Kane fell to a crouch. Better to get closer to their height. As he did, a pair of the creatures stood only feet away. No eyes that Kane could see, just those legs, and a mouth that looked prehistoric in its design, a gaping jagged hole designed for cutting and tearing.

The crouch position helped. If they dodged one of the shots, they sailed onto the next barrage. He kept twisting with the gun to make sure that none of them were attempting an end run. But he guessed they didn't have the requisite amount of brainpower to figure out that move.

And once again Kane noticed that he was talking to himself as he shot them. The dementia of a lone soldier fighting against the odds for his life.

"Come on, you little fucking bastards. Come on! Gonna blow every single goddamned one of you—"

His yelling incessant, the volume keeping up with the never-ending blasts of his gun. Until suddenly the trigger didn't do anything. No more rounds erupted from the muzzle: the damn thing needing to be reloaded. But how the hell could he reload with them—with them—

He looked up, expecting to see half dozen ready to jump on him.

But the floor was a sea of gore—legs sticking up at strange angles like the spiky tails of horseshoe crabs. He could see a few still twitching, but beyond that, nothing else.

He stayed crouched, waiting for his breathing to return to normal. He slowly dug out a fresh cartridge for his gun and clicked it into place. If he had been short a few more rounds, it would have been all over.

And when his breathing was fully back to normal, when the madness of his own voice yelling and the gunfire started receding from his brain, he stood up.

The way ahead was straight on through the hellish remains. As he started again walking forward, he ignored the crunch and bumps of the once-living horrors below his feet.

Maria stood back-to-back with Andy Kim.

"Okay," she said, not turning to him, "brace yourself. Here come some more of them."

The strategy of the zombies—and that's what they called them—seemed to consist of one thing. Come at a target from two different directions and attack with all the speed their mangled bodies could muster.

Some of them lumbered, but others, probably based on how the shock wave hit them, moved quite fast. Maybe even faster than they used to move. A few of the dead creatures at their feet had performed a dodging and weaving motion that momentarily made them a hard target.

"Hold on. Let's wait until they're a bit closer."

But Maria was no lieutenant, she knew, and her suggestion could be heard and ignored. And it was in this case.

"Fuck that!" Kim started blasting at the pair moving toward him. Maria guessed a good number of his shots went wide, especially if they were trying to dodge the fire. And it took a good number of bullets to bring them down. The supply of ammo on Mars couldn't be endless. And no telling if they were in this hell for the long haul.

So Maria held off until the trio of zombies coming toward her were only about ten meters away. One of them, she saw, seemed to have objects stuck to his body, things that moved when he moved. Was that a nail gun sticking out the side of one? Could the thing use it? And another had a heavy-duty industrial stapler embedded in its shoulder.

Nice folks to have over for dinner. Except in this case, she and Kim were the intended entrees.

"Okay," she whispered, more to herself than Kim, and she began firing at the three creatures now not too far away from her. Which is when she learned that the objects now part of their twisted bodies could still work. First the stapler started heaving on one of the thing's shoulder, spewing out thick staples onto the ground in front of the thing.

Not much of a weapon there.

But the other, with the nail gun, that was a different story. The gun started to shake and, like a feeble antenna, made an attempt to point. And it began firing out a stream of metal rivets. Most caromed off the metal wall, but when the creature bobbed and weaved, one or two actually came in her direction.

Bobbed and weaved, she thought. Not much different from being in the ring, when she had to watch the moves, the surprises an opponent had for her. Though they never brought mechanical tools into the ring.

She peppered both of them equally with gunshots, tattooing their chests with so many holes that the three of them should have fallen facedown a long time ago. But each of them had one more step in them before they fell.

Without turning, she spoke to Andy. "Corridor's getting a bit full.'

For a moment neither of them said anything. Then Andy: "How long you think we have to stay here? Hold down this fort, so to speak?"

"Not too sure. I'm hoping that the backup systems will kick in, we'll get a contact, find out what's happening elsewhere." She took a deep breath. "But until then, I think we have to wait a little longer. Make sure all the zombies trying to get past here have had their shot—and we've had ours."

"Time, Moraetes? Ten minutes?"

Maria hesitated. If they started moving, and if there were still waves of the things to come, then that would be a big mistake. But for now she said, "Sure. Ten minutes. Then we'll do a small recce. Deal?"

"Yeah."

And then they both went silent again while those minutes so slowly ticked away.

•　　　•　　　•

Kane now felt himself looking not only left and right with every step but up as well. No more surprises, he thought. Not like the last one.

Even when he stopped to check his PDA—as he did now—he would tap the screen with his thumb while quickly jerking his head up for another thorough scan, 360 degrees around, and up to the ceiling.

On the PDA he saw that just ahead should be a staircase. It looked narrow, but it did lead to one of the main corridors heading to the sector around Alpha.

Again he asked himself why he didn't just return to Reception. Make a last redoubt there. But he dismissed the idea just as quickly. *A last goddamn redoubt? You're already half-dead once you start thinking like that—you've half surrendered. And there's a good chance any enemy will know that.*

So just "returning there," waiting, praying, wasn't an option.

And then there was Maria—the boxer who, much like himself, acted, then sorted things out later. Or, as in both their cases, didn't sort out. They had a lot in common.

But, after another moment's thought, he knew it was something else.

How long had it been before anything really human had been in his life? Someone to help build a wall around the orders, the commands, the military, the chain of duty and events that had become his life?

Too goddamned long.

And once he admitted that, just that thought

seemed to open a door he had closed tightly. If Maria was alive, he knew he'd find her. And for now, that's all he needed to know.

Maria gave Andy Kim a nudge with her elbow. "Hear that?"

"Yeah. What the hell—"

"Shh—listen."

It had been quiet. Just the sound of them breathing deep, waiting, occasionally shifting their guns to the other shoulder. Both tired, thirsty, nearly half-mad with all the shooting. And the stench of the bodies just seemed to grow.

Andy broke the silence. "Damned if I know. Something deep. Then those smaller sounds, like—like—"

"Cats."

"What?"

"Like cats—I dunno—mewling, but like someone recorded the sound, raised it up a few octaves."

"More like screams."

"Exactly."

Again silence.

"Think whatever it is is coming this way?'

"Doubt we'll have long to wait."

The metal stairway door cantilevered to the side; one bottom corner actually dug into the floor. Grabbing and pulling on it told Kane that sheer strength wasn't going to do a thing here.

He turned and looked at the area around the door. A sign announced: ONLY AUTHORIZED LAB PERSONNEL ARE PERMITTED IN THIS AREA. PLEASE SHOW YOUR IDENTIFICATION TO THE SECURITY GUARD.

The guard? That must be the ripped-up pieces of bone and flesh lying by the wall.

But Kane also noticed that a table—perhaps the security guard's—had been turned over and one metal leg snapped off where it had been bolted to the tabletop.

He grabbed it and gave it a heft, checking its strength as best he could. It seemed to hold up. Kane turned back to the door, wedged the metal piece in the open door top, and then began pulling on the other end of the leg.

At first it did nothing. But then he heard a small groan. Maybe the hinges freeing up? And the sound was enough for him to redouble his efforts, planting one foot—with his knee screaming in protest at the angle—and using his entire body weight.

Another groan, then a sharp snapping sound as the door lost the battle. A final loud snap, and the top half of the door tipped forward.

It still blocked the stairway, but there was a big enough opening at the top that Kane could hoist himself up and crawl into the other side. But before he did that, he noticed that the stairway was dark. Again, another failure of Mars City's emergency lighting.

A nice narrow dark stairway.

Maybe there's another way? he thought. *Fuck it. . . .*

He reached up, gun slung to his back, muzzle down, and as if he were in Quantico again, running through the rookie training ground, he climbed up the sheer piece of metal in front of the stairway and whatever awaited him.

23

"SHIT. I SEE SOMETHING," SAID ANDY KIM.

Maria felt his fear as though it were a living thing standing next to them. She was about to say something when she noticed a shape down at the other end of the hallway she had her eyes locked on.

"More goddamn zombies," Kim said.

But Maria, seeing the shape of what was coming toward her, knew it was no zombie. It was way too tall, too broad. *What we have here,* she thought, *is something completely different entirely.* Some new friends coming out to play.

Then the thing became more visible, and it looked like something out of some boys' superhero vid. A head shaped like a bullet, skin catching the light like gray armor, and no eyes.

"What the—"

Then the creature at Maria's end disappeared.

"Wait a sec—" Maria said. "Mine just vanished."

"Mine too. Was it even real? Did we—" Andy laughed, the sound forced. "Did we scare them away?"

The thing appeared right in front of her, not all

at once, but slowly, as if being squeezed out of one place and into this foul corridor. And even before it was fully there, she began firing. She used the same pattern as before, but the shells seem to disappear into the armorlike skin, not ricochet.

As if the creature could just absorb them.

And only feet away.

She kept thinking: *It has no eyes.* Then: *But it does have a mouth, everything here gets a mouth. Mouths must not be optional.*

Andy Kim's voice passed hysterical and he yelled out his words. "Nothing's happening! It just keeps coming!"

"Target the mouth. Just aim there!"

Maria had already stopped trying to kill the creature with shots where a heart should be but probably wasn't. Her shots arced up from the chest to the mouth cavity already opening, teeth a dark brown, shimmering with something viscous. But now her bullets blasted into that mouth. The creature stopped, then took a step back.

As if filling a bucket, Maria kept pouring in the bullets, until the thing attempted to vanish.

Only this time it was halfway gone when the upper torso, now unsupported by legs that already had been sucked back to wherever the hell they came from, fell to the floor.

The half-creature tried to use its arms to scurry after Maria—a last-ditch attempt to get at her. Instead, what was left of it fell at her feet.

She heard Andy gag, and spun around to see a tall creature suspending him in the air with one hand, its brown teeth close to his skull as if getting ready to bite a juicy apple. The other hand was in motion, heading right toward Andy's midsection.

Maria didn't waste any shots on the thing's body, and she could only hope that her aim in close quarters would be good enough.

Andy's eyes met hers, and the emptiness she saw there, as opposed to wild panic, showed that he had already submitted to the death that was come. Probably only begging that it be fast.

Maria fired a long blast at the thing's head, some of the shots actually entering the mouth cavity from her side angle.

Then she jammed her gun in front of her, trying to knock the creature's other hand from hitting Andy's middle and—in all likelihood—ripping it open.

As soon as the gunmetal hit the creature's claw in motion, she felt how much power was behind it. Still, her strong hold caused the claw to deflect. The other claw could still close like a pincer around Andy's neck. Maybe—a stray thought suggested— there was some reason they wanted their prey alive and kicking before being devoured. If that was what it intended to do.

The creature's free claw closed around the muzzle of the gun. And though Maria didn't know she was going to do this, she let the gun go free.

Some tiny bit of consciousness she hadn't even

been aware of noticed that Andy's gun had fallen to the floor after he was grabbed.

She fell to her knees, as if performing a strange, violent religious ritual; she looked and aimed upward, now with an even better angle at the creature's mouth. Andy's eyes were closed. Blacked out, or . . . ?

She just kept the trigger pulled as a seemingly endless stream of bullets flew into the creature's maw. Then—like a bear trap springing free—the claw released Andy's neck. Andy fell hard to the floor and didn't move. The creature turned, slowly, stuff now erupting out of its mouth.

She noticed that it wasn't just fluid. There were things embedded in the stream, chunks of things. All she could do was stay on her knees before this monster god and keep firing until there wasn't a single bullet left.

And when that happened, it corresponded to the moment the creature's stream of bile stopped. Then—an amazing moment—it too buckled at the knees and came to an almost mirror-duplicate position of Maria's.

They faced each other, one dead, one alive.

And to finish the ceremony, Maria used the butt-end of her gun to push the creature backward, ending the services . . . for now.

Kane shut off his light. How long could it work if he left it on all the time? Two hours, three? Even here, in the fabled Mars City, a battery was a battery. He'd need to find some more flashlights, more ammo, and—

Better weapons . . .

If his instinct was right, he didn't know what was ahead. And not knowing put him, the marines, and the entire UAC at a distinct disadvantage.

He hoped that—with the light off—his eyes might adjust to the gloom, using whatever bits of scant light that seeped in, but there didn't seem to be any glimmers anywhere.

The darkness was near total, like a coffin interior six feet under.

He had both hands extended at his sides to feel the wall as he tentatively took the stairs step by step, feeling each step edge with his boot, then climbing up. It was so dark he thought that the only way he'd know he reached the top of the stairs would be when he either bumped into the door ahead (and there had to be a door, no?) or tried to find the next step and felt only a flat metal obstruction.

No magic night vision appeared to his eyes.

That was another tool he could use. Night goggles, some explosives, a few thermite grenades. A few? A dozen maybe. A chain gun, but he didn't even know whether they had them up here. A rocket launcher wouldn't be bad either.

Of course, there was no way to carry all that unless he found a nice cart to pull somewhere, making him look like a small-time weapons peddler. That image made him grin.

•   •   •

Maria cradled Andy's head. Amazingly, he was still breathing. But she couldn't get his eyes open. He needed a stim injection. Maybe more than one. Did she have any?

Maria gently lay his head down on the metal floor and turned to her side pack. She hadn't planned for combat when this day started. A stim pack wasn't something you usually patrolled Mars with, not when they could get a full infirmary team to you within five minutes. Every rookie removed the needles to make room for other stuff. Gum, pictures from home, a bit of hard-wired tech to watch vids or listen to music on the side.

She was sure that she had removed hers. But she dug through her pack, coming up empty-handed, then through Andy's. She found a few pics in his. Another space marine she had seen, a cute guy who worked the transport run. Interesting—Kim had never said a word.

But no stim needles.

"Damn," she thought. She'd have to leave Andy and go find them. Won't that be fun.

But just as she was about to get up and use her PDA to find where the nearest military storeroom was, she heard something. A bang. Then another. Something . . . down there. *Christ*, she thought, *doesn't this ever let up?*

She clicked a new cartridge into place in Andy's gun. She took a breath, stood up, and waited.

The twin banging noises were followed by a groaning sound, metal protesting against being moved. Maria gave her shoulders a shake—a boxer's move, getting loose and ready for the assault. Only now, all alone, ready was one thing she didn't feel at all.

24

THEO RAN TOWARD THE LIGHTS AHEAD. *Maybe there will be real people there*, he thought. He had dodged some of the others, the ones who looked all twisted, as if something had melted them. Now as he ran he heard noises behind him.

Not the heavy steps of the things that used to be soldiers, but a light tapping against the metal floor. He kept pumping, but he decided to risk glancing back . . . and he saw what was running after him so fast.

Bugs. At least, they looked like bugs, or spiders of some kind. A lot of them, right on his heels.

He started to pump his arms harder, as if somehow that could make his legs move faster. He told himself—warned himself—*Don't slip*. One slip, and in seconds they would be on him.

(And what would they do, what would they do to him?)

Don't think of that either, he thought. And so he kept looking at the light, now not so far away, not knowing where he was or where the light led to or even if it was a good or bad thing. He just kept sprinting as fast as he could.

Maria looked down at Andy. *One good thing about his being out cold—if it ends here, he'll miss it.*

And she had to wonder: *Is it something I should miss too? Instead of letting them get me? It could all be over so fast. . . . No, screw that,* she thought. She hadn't come this far—literally—to take her own life.

The thing at the end of the hall was a dark, hulking shape. A solitary figure now moving toward her.

She raised her weapon, ready for the next attack, finger tight on the trigger.

The bright lights seemed to be at the end of the hallway. Theo thought that he was trapped, like when he'd play hide-and-seek with the kids from school, and somehow you ended up in an alleyway where there was no place to go. No place to run.

But as he hit the corner, he saw that the hallway turned left, then went straight a bit more, where he saw . . .

A train. No—what were they called? A monorail! Like at the theme park they went to. He saw it sitting there, the door open. Was it broken? Did somebody need to come and get it running again?

He could still hear the chatter of the legs on metal closer now.

He ran into the open monorail car and pressed against the wall. Only when he was inside did he notice the big red smears that went from the floor to the wall. He stepped away from the splotches to the front of the monorail car. His hands felt behind him as he did.

Then Theo saw the spider things hit the same corner he had just come from. In only seconds they'd be there, ready to climb into the car and trap him.

A voice from above, over the internal speaker system. *"Monorail D2 is preparing to depart."*

A chance for escape . . . but would it leave in time? From his angle, Theo could see outside, waiting for the first spider-creature to reach the open door.

Then the soothing voice again. *"Attention: Monorail now departing for Delta Labs. Please hold on."*

He saw the first spider arrive. It didn't see the monorail, the open door. He forced himself to be still while he waited for the door to shut, so horribly slowly creeping to a closed position.

Another spider . . . Theo saw the narrow heads on top of the insectile body.

The two of them outside finally turned, seeing the monorail and the opening, shifting, rearing back, and Theo knew they were going to leap in. But the door had only inches left to close. In that moment when they pulled back to leap into the car, the door finally shut.

And the calm, soothing voice came back as the monorail left this place.

"Please hold on during our journey to Delta Labs. Thank you, and have a nice day in Mars City."

Theo's heart pumped. Had he touched something to make it go, or did it just go, back and forth between the place he had been and the place he was going to?

And what would be waiting for him at the other end of this trip?

Maria licked her lips. *Time to start blasting—fill the thing with holes and see what stops it. And do that to the next one, and the one after that, on and on. My new job. Until I'm the last one left, until here is no more ammo. My own private little Alamo.*

Her finger tightened. Then a bit of light from her end caught the front of the body walking to her. She noticed again how its gait wasn't like the others', that confused step of something mastering a new skill.

It walked like a human.

She hesitated, and then as more light came into the hallway, she saw that it was indeed human. A space marine who hadn't been put through the meat grinder of whatever happened here. Then a few more steps, and she recognized the face.

She whispered the word to herself at first: "Kane." Then louder, coming out of her crouch: "Kane!"

And Maria couldn't remember feeling quite as good in a very long time.

Theo looked out the window as the monorail went into a stone tunnel. Lights made the surrounding redbrick glow. Then the track quickly curved up, climbing a bit, before leveling off.

Where did it say it was going? Delta Labs? Was that a good place to be going?

He pressed his face against the glass. Maybe there would be people there to take care of him.

The stone tunnel changed to all metal. *"Approaching Delta Labs. Please make sure to take all your belongings with you and have your Security IDs ready."*

No belongings, no ID. So Theo just waited.

25

KANE AND MARIA STOOD LOOKING AT EACH other without saying a word for what seemed like a long time. Then she took a step closer to him, and he knew that the silence was born of the awareness that—standing here in this corridor filled with death—they both had seen and done things that could never be erased from their minds, things that they both might never be able to talk about.

And perhaps the idea that this was far from over.

And with that awareness, Kane watched Maria do something so unexpected but at the same time something that felt perfectly natural.

She leaned forward and kissed him.

It had been so long. Kane stood still, unsure about what to do. But then his arms, bruised and battered as they were, went around Maria and pulled her tight. And after that kiss, they just stood there, holding each other tight, the human contact so good.

But even as Kane hugged her back hard, his eyes kept peering past her, down one end of the corridor, and he hoped that she was doing the same.

Until finally, reluctantly, they let their clinch go, and Maria moved away from him.

Kane smiled. "So where did that come from?"

And Maria smiled back. "Maybe I'm just glad you're not one of them."

"Me too."

"Hm?"

"I'm glad *you're* not one of them also."

Slowly, even more reluctantly, they let the moment pass. There were things to do if they were to stay alive.

Maria started: "Look, Andy here had a run-in with this big thing. No eyes that I could see. Armor skin."

"Yeah, one of them nearly got me."

"What the hell is it?"

Kane held up his PDA. "No communication from the front office on that question. No—what's the word?—'memo' on what to call them."

"They seem to be able to appear, and vanish."

"Noticed that too."

"I had a book once where something did that . . . called an imp."

"Bet it wasn't that big."

She laughed. "Or that ugly. Still—"

"'Imp' it is, then. Good to name these things. I also ran into something new." A breath. "Actually more than one. Spiderlike things, or like a giant mite, the size of a dog. They had this head emerging from the top. Not actually a head, almost a small torso—like two creatures in one."

"How about 'trite'?"

Kane smiled. "'Trites.' Good. So when you find yourself in a room full of them, you can say, 'Got a lot of goddamn trites here.'" He looked down at the man on the floor. "Is he . . . dead? Or one of them now?"

"No. That's Andy Kim. Stood by me when things just kept coming. The imp had him, and he's unconscious. I don't have my stim packs. Everyone dumps them."

Kane started digging around in his small side pack. "Not a newbie. I've used one myself." He pulled out the small wrapped syringe. "You want to do the honors?"

Maria took the pack, ripped open the top, and took out the needle. "Don't know much about first aid, so this might not even be good for him."

"Probably better than lying on the floor here, waiting."

"Right."

Maria removed the cap that covered the needle end and brought the needle close to Andy's carotid artery. She had heard that the best thing to do was shoot it right into the artery. She looked up at Kane.

"Sure you don't want to do this? You must have seen the training vid more recently than me."

Kane held out his hands, bloody, bruised, and banged—probably clumsy things even when not all messed up.

"I think you best proceed, Doctor."

She pressed the needle into a spot below the line made by the vein. The chemical cocktail of the stim hypo should hit Andy fast, and he'd either be able to get up or not.

The needle pushed the skin in—she could see it stretch a bit. Then more pressure, and the needle punctured. A small bloom of blood surrounded the thin stem of the needle. Maria kept her hands as steady as she could, her thumb on the small plunger, and then slowly began to press down.

She kept her eyes on Andy's, waiting for some sign of reaction. His chest showed him breathing with a steady rise and fall. But she wanted to see the stim do its stuff, have Andy's eyes pop open, and then a smile and he'd be back.

The plunger was almost fully pressed.

"Damn. Nothing," she said quietly.

"Give it a second," Kane added. "Could take time."

The small syringe was empty, and now she gingerly pulled the needle out as a small pool of blood formed at the opening.

"Need a bandage. I got one in—"

But Kane had anticipated that and handed her one of the small cotton swatches from his pack. Maria took it and pressed it against the opening. Kane stood by with a bit of plastic tape. She took that, sealing the bandage in place.

"Maybe . . . we should try another. Maybe he's so far gone it will take two."

And when she had just about convinced herself

that another still had to be tried, Andy's chest swelled with a big gulp of air. His mouth opened and then, as if someone had thrown a switch, his eyes popped open, darting left and right, as if the last thing he remembered was the imp's claw hand around his neck, and he expected the creature to be there.

But Maria cleared some hair off his forehead and she smiled. And after the nervous dance of his eyes back and forth, Andy relaxed, the slow realization that he was alive, and that he was safe, hitting his now conscious brain.

And Maria said, "Welcome back."

Theo hesitated before the open monorail door. Would it close again in a few seconds, and would he travel back to the other place?

Where the spiders waited. . . .

He placed one foot right where the door would slide shut, still undecided.

Then the voice came back: *"The monorail is ready for departure. Please hold on."*

And with that, Theo stepped out. As soon as he did, the door whooshed closed behind him. He could hear the voice inside, talking to nobody.

The monorail pulled away, leaving Theo alone, unsure of what his next move would be, beyond not staying in one place for very long.

Andy Kim leaned again the wall, nodding and smiling. "I got to tell you . . . I thought it was all over. I was"—he looked at Kane—"actually glad that I was blacking out." Then his eyes looked straight ahead. "I sure didn't want to be conscious to see what that thing would do to me."

Kane didn't know how Maria was trained to deal with combat fatigue of any sort. In truth, he barely knew her. But he could see in Kim the telltale signs of shock. In this unfocused state, Kim wasn't going to be any good to them at all.

And that was important, because since reaching Maria the question kept dogging him even as he pushed it to the back of his mind: what next?

He would have liked to pull Maria aside, discuss Kim and a potential plan. But the young space marine was already freaked-out enough. He likely didn't need any secret discussions happening around him. So Kane decided to lay the cards on the table.

"Okay, well, glad you're alive, Andy. I ran into two of those—"

"Imps," Maria said. Then she shrugged, as if recognizing it was a pretty feeble name for such a creature.

Kane repeated the name with a smile, "Okay, imps. They're definitely not, as we say, from here. And I've seen two other things, also not zombies."

Andy said, "Two? I know about that doglike thing with metal hindquarters. That picture got out to all the marines before the comm failure. But there's another?"

Kane nodded. "That I've seen . . . that I know of.

Didn't grab any pictures of them—too busy blowing them away to play zoologist. Or more appropriately, entomologist. They were spiderlike, size of dogs. The legs were either some hard body material—I dunno—maybe metal legs like the pinky." He looked at Maria. "We're calling them 'trites' since they looked a bit like mites but were massive."

"Trites . . ." Andy repeated.

"Okay, also not much of a name. But I'll tell you"—he looked down at Andy—"one thing I learned leading grunts into battle is, if you can mock the goddamn enemy, then go ahead and do it. Make them small so it seems like, yeah, you can take them out. You can beat them. So if we're talking about imps, trites, pinkies . . . so be it. These creatures don't need names that actually sound dangerous."

Maria nodded. "Right. Good idea. Next one we meet we'll call a 'clown.' "

Kane laughed. "How many clowns did you kill today." He turned back to Andy, who, in the pattern of shock, had quickly drifted away.

Kane crouched down. "So, Andy, I've been cooking up a little plan. I want to get you out of here. Things are quieter back at Reception. It's close to transport when help comes—"

Kane knew he wasn't being completely truthful with Kim. Things had been quieter back there. But now? It was anybody's guess. And help? Had help been summoned? Not the last time Kane was there. And that was another part of his plan. . . .

But that wasn't for Andy Kim's ears.

"So I'm going to have Maria take you back. You can join up with the grunts I left there. There's a guy, McCullough. Pain in the ass, but he has a good head on his shoulders. No brass around, so I put him in charge."

Andy nodded, and Kane thought it was all settled.

Maria took some steps so she could look at Kane. "And you? What are you going to do?"

He stood up, hoping that Kim would drift away. While he didn't walk away from the man, he turned a bit and lowered his voice. "Far as I can tell, all of this is coming from one place, and even being new to this wonderful city, I can tell that's Delta Lab."

"And?"

"Now that I know you're safe, and things look a little quiet here, that's where I'm going to go. The way I figure it, if our menagerie is coming from there, somebody better close the damn gate."

"Right. Only one thing: you can't go alone."

"Hm?"

"You said you had a hard time getting here, whole sections blocked, elevators down, stairways clogged. Do you think you know Mars City well enough to get to Delta on your own?"

Kane waved his PDA at her. "I got maps."

"Yeah, and you are a smart marine. So you know maps don't show everything. You need me to get there."

"I'll be okay. Maybe hit a few dead ends. Won't be the first time."

She reached out and touched his arm. "And there's this: you came here to see if I was okay, if I needed help. Well, you damn sure know you'll need help when you get to Delta. The words 'suicide mission' seem apt."

"Possibly."

"And it might be less of a suicide mission if I go with you."

"Or maybe we'll both die."

She smiled and repeated the same word he had just said to her: "Possibly. But you know I'm right."

Kane had to admit that she had a strong point. Any other marine he'd order to go with him, bringing as much firepower as possible. Funny how other . . . factors . . . can cloud one's judgment.

He flicked his head toward Kim. "And Andy?"

"You said you know a clear path back to Reception. Hopefully you've taken care of all the monsters who have come out to play along that route."

"Not sure about that."

"We give Andy another one of your stims. Get him up. And get him moving."

He looked down at Kim, still leaning against the wall, eyes glazed, staring out at the distance.

"You give him a chance of making it back?"

"Maybe. Maybe not. But it's that—"

Then, in a raspy voice from below Kane: "I can do it."

He watched Kim press his back against the wall

and start to slide up to a standing position. "I can do it. On my own." On his two feet now, he looked at Kane. "You show me exactly how you got here, and"—he turned to Maria—"you load me up with all the ammo and stim I can handle, and I can do it. McCullough, you say?"

Andy's last words seemed designed to convince Maria that he was really all right to handle this.

"Andy, are you sure—?"

Then a smile, warm and so human, and now even Kane believed that the kid could make it back. "I can do it. Kane, you have to take her. Who knows what the hell is going on here, but if it's going to be stopped, there's a better chance with two of you."

Kane nodded. "Yeah. Too right on that. Okay, then I guess we all better get started. Before we break up, we need ammo, all that we can carry. And there's got to be some grenades around here. Some backup weapons. Any autoload shotguns?"

Maria nodded. "We can get all that pretty near here."

Andy took a breath. "Then, let's get that stuff and get going." He looked back and forth between the two of them. "Enough talking, right?"

Kane nodded. "Right."

Though he knew that once he and Maria began their trek, he would have to tell her everything he felt about what was happening here. That, and what he planned to do about it. But that was for the two of them. For now he just said," Lead on."

And Maria picked up her weapon and led them down a supply corridor to what he hoped would be the largest cache of guns and ammo he had ever seen.

Theo heard little pops and clicks from somewhere on the monorail platform, but that sounded electrical. Nothing out of the ordinary—nothing from the things that used to be human.

He was starving, ravenous; and when he gulped, he could feel how thirsty he was. *I need water and food,* he thought. *I need help. I need somebody to help me.*

Of course, calling out wasn't something he could do. No, not when it was so quiet and his voice would be the only thing here. *The only human thing. . . .*

Where am I? Theo wondered. *Is this a good place, a bad place? Why is it so quiet?* The hunger, the thirst, nagging at him.

He had stood there as long as he could. And without knowing where he might be going, he started moving, one step at a time, his destination a complete unknown.

26

JULIE POINTED TO THE SCREEN IN FRONT OF David.

"Okay, this is what I've been looking at. This process. We always called it symbiotic, toxin-eating bacteria producing food for the organic host. But now it doesn't add up."

David leaned close; the clarity was perfect, with the microcamera's ability to record in startling 3-D the moment-by-moment process of the formation of that bond between organic and inorganic.

"Can I see it again? Maybe let the image rotate as it goes on? I'd like to see a three-sixty view."

"Sure. Hold on."

Julie hit some keys, and the video, enlarged at a magnification of 1200X, began again, this time with the "camera" actually rotating around the molecules as they did their work.

"Hold on. Okay. Stop it there."

David hesitated for a moment. He tapped the screen to indicate where a new section of bacteria seemed to appear out of nowhere. "Can you enlarge that? Maybe another five hundred times?"

Julie glided a small pointer over the screen, and then she stroked a slide bar to bring the image up to a close-up at the higher power.

"See there?"

"You mean the bacteria first growing, spreading, then—"

"Look. Right there. Looks like it's planting some kind of hooks into the host material. Doesn't look very symbiotic to me."

"You're right. We missed that. Until we had the molecules at this early stage, the exact nature of the process remained a bit of guesswork. Like physicists' speculation about what happened in those microseconds before and after the Big Bang."

"Exactly. But what we have here is the Big Bang equivalent of a totally new form of existence." He turned and looked at Julie. "And doesn't something about it bother you?"

She hesitated. He knew that Julie was never one to go with instinct. That would have been too classically female. She was all logic, even when it came to their relationship. That may have been the thing that ended it. "I don't know. I guess you could say that it looks . . . aggressive?"

"Exactly."

"But without the bacteria moving and taking

over, the host organism couldn't even exist, not in the hydrothermal vents."

"True. But at what price? Or to put it another way, who is actually the host, and who the creature? And if we are to actually play with this material, somehow try to master this process for human use . . ."

"Which won't be done in the next day, or even week—"

"You can be sure of that. That's the first thing Kelliher has to hear. But we have to learn everything we can. Quite frankly, watching this . . . worries me."

Again Julie was reluctant to express such an unscientific thought. "I can see that. We have more tests running, with different samples, different conditions, and we—"

The intercom came on. "Dr. Rodriguez, the first visitors are here."

Visitors—some of the scientists that Kelliher had dispatched here immediately after the first outbreak, ferried here via a transport chopper. The subs and a docking ship waited for them on the surface. And with many more scientists to come.

They'd need briefing assignments, all the formalities of finding a place for them to live and work down here on what might be a total pipe dream.

David would have to show them the images, the vids. That is, if Kelliher hadn't already sent them some of the material from Mars.

"Company," he said to Julie. "I best get them sorted. You okay to carry on?"

She nodded. He started to turn to walk away, but Julie, in an almost impulsive gesture, reached out and touched his left forearm.

"David, it's good that I can go over all this with you. Helps my thinking."

He nodded. "I wouldn't want it any other way. Call me any time, any hour, when you have something." Then, with her hand still on her arm, he said, "Or even if you don't."

She nodded and smiled back.

"I better dash."

And he hurried up to the entry dock to wait for the first submersibles to arrive.

UAC Headquarters
Palo Alto

"Would you like an escort down to the labs, Mr. Kelliher?"

The UAC chairman waved away the question from the security officer. He knew his the way around the labs below—after all, he had approved every piece of the design. And he wanted as much time alone with his thoughts as possible.

He kept running his plans through his head, second-guessing the twisted path of thoughts that led him to the conclusions that he had to do . . . what he was about to do.

Amazing, he thought, *the power of fear.*

The elevator doors shut smoothly, and the elevator began the long journey belowground to the only other "floor" it went to. The service elevators, of different sizes, went to various access levels above and below the labs.

But for this one, direct from the headquarters building, there was only one stop.

No, he thought, there was no question that he had to do this. Though, God knew, the risks were tremendous. Could this be one roll of the dice too many for the UAC? And how long before the government, as enfeebled and indebted to the UAC as it was, decided that the time had come to sever the relationship?

Sever it, and perhaps even more. Could they attempt to take over the UAC? And how would he, Ian Kelliher, react to that? Or rather, how should he react? If anything, the ineffectiveness of what passed for the United States government was something that drove all of the UAC's operations.

The elevator slowed. The door opened. And two armed guards, though they certainly knew who was standing in front of them, lowered their weapons to chest height and demanded to see Kelliher's security pass, to be followed by a retinal scan follow-up.

He walked out of the elevator and handed them his UAC security card.

David Rodriguez watched the screen in the transport area as it signaled that the sub outside had successfully docked with the Ballard station.

The sub's airlock opened, and then both computer systems performed a check of air quality and pressure. Then with the slightest whoosh of air, the airlock opened. David took a few steps closer as the first scientists walked off.

Three of them, with more on the way. Drawn from cutting-edge projects in genetic adaptation, molecular biophysics, and other related fields.

Two of them middle-aged, fitting the scientific mold. And one striking redhead.

Dr. Elaina Krasanov, whose plant-specific work in genetic modifications had been touted—in scientific circles at least—as a way to end the food wars that raged all over the earth. Of course, that still wouldn't deal with the water problem. But supposedly her recent plant modifications could grow in near-desert conditions, absorbing even the scant moisture from the air itself.

All that—and it was hard not to look at her.

The scientists stood there, looking around the transport bay.

David wanted to give this group a quick orientation and get them working as soon as possible.

"Gentlemen . . . and lady, welcome to the Robert Ballard Deep Ocean Lab. I know you have all been briefed on what we are doing now. And the new urgency of the project."

The group looked at each other, and David now knew that they had indeed seen the images and vids from Kelliher and had had a thorough briefing on where David and his team were with the project.

"My lead scientist here, Dr. Julie Chao, will see to your formal orientation in the lab. I'm afraid we've made no distinct assignments. We prefer that you see all the areas we are working on, then, where you see a fit, you can jump in."

David smiled, but didn't see any smiles back. Probably the looseness of the organization was clearly not to their liking.

"Bottom line: if you see an area we are working on where there is a good fit, we'd like . . . we *need* you to simply join the team. In some cases, you may actually end up running the team. But with this crisis, such designations don't matter. Before I take you to the lab, and we begin—any questions?"

One hand went up, a man whose face looked familiar.

"Dr. Rodriguez, you have used the word 'urgent.'" The man looked at the others. "And we of course have seen the possible threat. The situation on Mars. But I—and a few of the others—would like to know why you—and perhaps Ian Kelliher—feel that the situation is urgent, and our work is needed to produce results quickly."

David nodded. "Thanks for that question. And I can only say that the fear is that what is going on up there . . . might not be confined to Mars."

"But how—" another scientist started to say.

David held up a hand. "I know. Mars is far away.

But you see, there is one thing that drives this work now. The UAC, the survivors on Mars who—as you know—are now facing a second 'outbreak,' don't have a clue what happened there." David took a breath. "And if not knowing doesn't pose an immediate threat to us, even here on Earth, well, I don't know what does."

He saw Dr. Krasanov look at him, a hint of a smile on her lips. Beyond her scientific accomplishments, there were other stories about the fiery redhead. David looked away from her eyes—a dark piercing green—and scanned the scientists.

"Other questions, please ask me at any time. For now—some of my assistants will take your bags to your quarters. All doubled up, I'm afraid. Going to be a bit crowded down here."

"Me too?" Krasanov said, with just a hint of her St. Petersburg accent.

David shook his head. "No. For now at least. But there will be other female scientists joining us."

He turned back to his two assistants and nodded.

"So if you're ready, I will take you to our main lab." David turned, and started to lead. Then he looked back and said, "And good luck to us all."

27

IAN KELLIHER WALKED INTO THE LABS, AND
the scientists stood at attention. He had, of course,
sent them all the data and images from Mars. To
say that they now looked rattled was an understatement.

Dr. Silvio Adoni, leader of the team here, walked
over. "Mr. Kelliher. Sorry, we didn't expect a visit. Is
there anything you want—"

Kelliher cut off the apology. "That's fine, Silvio. I
came down because I wanted to speak with you and
the whole team."

Adoni, Kelliher knew, wasn't Betruger's equal,
though the lab here attempted to replicate what was
going on in Mars City. And it did—up to a point.
The long-range live experiments had never been attempted.

One reason the teleportation work was being done

on Mars was that, for something so revolutionary—
and so controversial—it was better to have the work
take place in as remote a location as possible. But
that was then. . . .

"I'll want to talk with everyone else in a few minutes. But first, perhaps a few words between us."

Adoni looked back at the others nervously. No,
definitely no Betruger here. Smart, perhaps even
a bit brilliant. But when Kelliher said jump, Adoni
asked how high.

"Should I tell them to get back to work, or—?"

"No. Have them come here." Kelliher put his arm
around the scientist and led him off to the side. "Silvio, I imagine that you can guess what I might be
about to say to you, to the team here?"

Adoni began to open his mouth, taking a big
breath, obviously reluctant to answer.

"Relax. It's not a damn quiz. I need this lab to try
and find out what happened up there—what's happening now, even as we speak. And I don't think we
have a lot of time."

Adoni nodded. Kelliher was sure that Adoni saw
this coming.

"I know it goes against some things we talked
about, that you might even feel uncomfortable about
it. But I need you leading it. Full speed ahead to get
answers as quickly as you can." Kelliher placed his
hand on the man's wrist. "I need to know that I can
depend on you to do what must be done. To ask no
questions and simply do the experimental work that

must be done. Immediately. So—" Kelliher took a breath. "I need an answer. Can you do that for me?"

Adoni looked right back at Kelliher, his eyes locked on him, clearly understanding what was being asked. The answer, when it came, would mean he knew what he was getting into.

"Well?"

"I will, Mr. Kelliher. I—I'll lead the project. Even with the rules we had in place . . . removed."

Kelliher smiled and stood up. "Good. Let me talk with everyone, then."

SOMEWHERE BENEATH THE SURFACE OF MARS

Dr. Axelle Graulich looked down at her last canister of air. Mere minutes left, and then she would have nothing to breathe. She looked at the small device clipped to the side of her EVA suit that recorded current temperature and air quality. It showed that if she took off her helmet, she would be dead in seconds.

Only then did she look into the steadily increasing madness that was this opening.

The time when she had been the lead scientist investigating Site 3 seemed a lifetime ago instead of mere hours, a time that left the rest of her team dead from the shock waves, and sent her plummeting into what at first seemed like a stone tunnel dug out of the hard red stone of Mars.

Dug out . . . by someone.

As she walked, she looked at the carvings that covered the walls: symbols, words, all defying—for now—any understanding, any interpretation. Would anyone else ever see this cave of wonders? Would anyone ever record the images, try to decipher the message here?

She had heard a second blast minutes ago, so much bigger than the first one. But nothing more than a distant rumble reached down here.

At one point, she had been scared. After all, the cave walls and floor seemed to glow, as if slick with sweat, slimy, alive. But her feet left no impression in the claylike floor. As for the walls, she wasn't foolish enough to touch them.

And why did she keep walking? What other choice did she have?

Behind her, only dead soldiers and scientists. And no way to get up to the surface. And somehow this tunnel seemed naturally to lead deeper and deeper, under the skin of the Red Planet.

It would all be a moot point soon, when her air was gone. This strange mausoleum, with its glowing stone and symbols, would become her grave.

That was the other thing. The luminescence. She was unable to see where it came from, or even if it was true light. A soft deep-red glow suffused everything.

She'd love to send pictures and words back to Mars City. But there was no communication signal—hadn't been since the first blast. No, this tunnel was simply for her alone to experience, to try to understand, but understand with no chance of passing along her observations.

She did have her PDA. That was an idea. She could talk into her PDA, in case anyone ever came down here to look for her. They'd find her PDA—that would be something.

As much as she didn't want to, she looked back at the air canister's meter, now showing a minute, maybe two, left of sweet air to breathe.

Kelliher looked around the room, then spoke.

"Thank you for all the work you have done up to now. Each and every one of you have had to accept sacrifices to work here, with all that you do secret, the hours grueling, long. And now, I am here to ask more."

How many of them could guess what was coming next?

"You all have seen what has happened in Dr. Betruger's lab. I know that those images must appear disturbing, frightening . . ."

The wide eyes looking back told Kelliher he was more than right on that score.

"Now, with a second outbreak, and communications down, we don't know what is going on up there. Going on . . . or how to stop it. And so, after consulting with Dr. Adoni, I have made a decision."

He looked over at Adoni, who nodded at the lie that this was their plan.

"Commencing immediately, this lab will—at an accelerated rate—attempt to replicate the recent experiments of Delta Lab. I will be asking for double shifts from all of you, and of course this entire complex will remain sequestered for the duration. But—to put it simply—all those experiments that we have quite purposely avoided . . . this lab will now undertake."

One of the scientists coughed. A bit of a protest?

"If any of you wish to quit the project, you may do so after some formalities relating to security. Neither I nor the UAC will hold that against you. But believe me that I think more than helping Mars may be at stake here."

He stood there for a moment; the room felt frozen, glacial. He had given them the opportunity to quit. He wondered how many would avail themselves of that opportunity.

"You can take the next twenty minutes or so to decide. But after that, the work must commence. I have made all the arrangements at headquarters to get everything you need." He nodded at that, letting the full implications sink in. "Everything."

Another pause. And even Kelliher felt shaken by what he was about to do, right here.

"Any questions?"

Nothing, then a voice. "Mr. Kelliher."

A man at the back of the room, hidden by the others in front of him. "Yes?"

"What about the nodes? The satellite labs? The

network? Will they remain online?" Then, to make the question perfectly clear: "Will they remain connected to your lab here?"

Kelliher felt Adoni looking over at him. This was something they hadn't discussed. But it was something that Kelliher had thought about.

"Yes." Nervous looks were exchanged by some of the team. "I can't tell what the trigger was, where the 'phenomenon'—if we can call it that—came from. So for now, yes. The 'nodes'—the network you have been using for your experiments—will remain intact. I will inform all the team leaders around the world of that fact. Any other questions?"

No one said anything. Kelliher felt as though he should say something like *and may God bless us all.* But he doubted very much that God was down here, half a mile under the California hills, and he certainly doubted that God was with his people on Mars, who remained cut off, incommunicado . . . and facing things that Kelliher couldn't even imagine.

28

KANE GAZED AT THE NOW OPEN STOREROOM filled with weapons. "Christmas on Mars," he said.

He picked up a large-bore, water-cooled shotgun. A great weapon—it could fire almost as an automatic, sending 5-centimeter shells blasting into whatever stood in your way. "I'll take one of these."

Maria reached up to a shelf, grabbed a few boxes of machine gun clips, and handed them to Andy. "What else would you like?"

Andy looked around. "Maybe half a dozen of these." He reached over and picked up some thermite grenades and started clipping them to his belt. "A bit heavy, but might come in handy."

"Yeah," Kane said. "Me, too." He started attaching as many of the grenades to his belt as he could find room for.

Maria handed him some machine gun clips. "Fill your pockets with these. They tend to go fast."

"I've noticed that."

Kane did a sweep of the room. He'd like to take the whole damn storeroom with them, but there were limits to how much they could carry before it started to get in the way of mobility.

"And I think we'll need some batteries." Luckily there were a few boxes of the narrow batteries for the micro-flashlights. They were supposed to be good for a day at full power. But who knew how long they had been sitting here. "Better grab a light for yourself," he said to Maria.

She took one from a shelf, checked that it worked, and then grabbed another and gave it to Kim.

"Anything else?"

Kane's handgun was fully loaded, and, he suspected, so was Maria's.

Kane looked over the shelves. "No chain guns. . . . Plasma weapons?"

Maria shook her head. "No. Not standard issue. The brass may have some, but I imagine they're already in play."

"By 'in play' you mean the other team could have them, ready to use them against us."

"Could be."

Kane brought the shotgun up and took a practice aim. Nice balance. It was a newer model than the one he had slogged through the streets of Terekstan with. "We'll be fine with these. I hope. Still, let's keep our eyes open."

"Right."

He wondered if he should have another go at getting Maria to head back with Andy Kim. If he was about to head into the epicenter of whatever hell had been unleashed on Mars, the odds of coming back were—as the saying went—slim to none.

"You should reconsider. Go back—"

"Kane, enough! We have a plan." She turned to Kim. "Andy, you sure you're okay?"

"I'm fine—but I have to agree with Kane."

She shook her head, and Kane again saw that getting Maria Moraetes to change her mind was a task that was well beyond him.

"Time to go, boys. We need to close the store and start moving."

Kim nodded, and Kane saw Maria put a hand on his shoulder. "Be safe, Andy. I want to see you when Kane and I come back. . . ."

"Yeah, and you two—don't take any chances," Andy replied. "If we get it together, I'll try to organize some marines to come in relief."

"Good, " Kane said. "But only if you are sure that Reception and Transport are secure."

Kim rubbed his neck, the bruise from the imp visible on his throat.

"Right. If I can, I will. And that guy you said I should find—"

"McCullough. A pain in the ass, but I imagine he might have a handle on things back there. Tell him I sent you, and give him whatever help he needs."

Andy Kim nodded. "You got it."

For a moment they hesitated, a strange, unknown future ahead for all three, something that Kane was sure that they each felt.

Maria broke the silence. "Time to go."

"Good luck," Kim said, turning away and walking back, following Kane's alternate route to Alpha.

"You, too," Kane said.

Then he turned to Maria. "On to Delta," he said. She nodded, and he saw her give her weapons a little heave, checking her balance. Then she started leading the way ahead.

Maria stopped. "That way is the monorail. Probably still running. If it has power."

"But not the way to go?"

She turned to Kane. "No. If you're right, if this all comes from whatever was going on in Delta Labs, the monorail could drop us right in the middle of it."

"But Sergeant Kelly is there. A well-fortified squad."

"Yeah. But maybe not."

She saw in Kane's eyes that she didn't have to elaborate. "So, we're going to actually move for a while *away* from Delta. This way"—she pointed down a narrow corridor—"circles around to the rear of Delta, back to the main reactor."

"Delta has its own reactor?"

A nod. "It needed it. Supposedly. From there, we can find an elevator or a stairway to Level 2. After that, it's a bit of a hill, but it leads to the rear entrance of Delta Lab. If something's happening there, if something's going on, we might be able to see it—"

"Before it sees us?"

"That's the plan."

"Okay, we should—"

Maria's earpiece made a scratching noise.

"Hear that?" she asked.

Kane nodded.

"Comm coming back maybe? God, maybe we don't have to do this."

They stood there. Another burst of static, but then nothing. And no human voices cut through the scratchy noise.

"Not back yet," Kane said.

Maria nodded. Some human voice would be good. Just so she didn't have to think it was maybe only the three of them left alive. Like that story, "Ten Little Indians," with the entire space marine company up here being whittled away, one by one.

"Okay. Maybe it will come back. Maybe it won't. Let's get moving."

"So tell me—what do you think is happening here?" Kane asked.

Maria looked up at him as they walked. This corridor was well lit by the emergency lights, giving it an almost safe feel. Light equals civilization, she thought. And probably has since the days when humans would huddle in caves by their fires, waiting for dawn to come.

"I think you're asking the wrong person. I mean, there were rumors. Some weird shit happened."

"Like what?"

She took a breath. "Well, for the past year some of the grunts on duty in Delta started losing it. They'd just snap, babbling about evil and demons. Some guys would fall to their knees babbling, praying; probably they were religious before they went in there. . . .".

"And they saw something that challenged their beliefs?"

"Yeah, probably. Even happened to some of the doctors. One I saw . . . was wheeled out of here to a transport in a straitjacket." She turned to him. "Can you believe that?"

"After what I've seen today? Yeah." Then Maria noticed Kane wince.

"You okay?"

He nodded. "Just some bangs to the knee. Nothing major."

"Need a stim?"

"Not now. Later." He took a breath, and she knew he was in more pain than he admitted. "And the rumors?"

"Ah—that was the interesting part. Stories about the experiments were all over the place, though nobody really knew what Dr. Betruger was working on. Top secret, everyone sworn not to say anything, under penalty of prosecution. Still . . . stories seeped out."

"Stories about—?"

"A new way to travel, perhaps a new engine that could really get us out of our own solar system to other star systems. That was one theory. Others about strange biological experiments that had to do with whatever happened to life on Mars. Most of those tales centered around Site 3."

"That's the excavation area that I saw."

"Yeah. A big cave, a lot of scientists working. Supposedly had nothing to do with the experiments Betruger was doing in the lab, but no one believed that. No one at all. Somehow they were linked. But who knew how?"

She looked at Kane and gave him a smile. "And there you have the sum total of my knowledge about what they've been up to in Mars City. Not very helpful, is it?"

"Still, good to know what everyone was— Oh, wait!" He stopped at an intersection. "I'm guessing we go left?"

And left, Maria saw, was pitch-dark. Completely black.

29

KANE PEERED INTO THE DARKNESS THAT seemed to stretch forever. Infinite blackness.

"We're going to need the lights," he said. "To point out the obvious." But his humor didn't ease the tension he felt in Maria.

"I just wish we had some major lights. Guess they figured with all the emergency backup, these small things"—she dangled the flashlight, not much larger than her hand—"would be all we need."

"At least we have them, and lots of batteries."

"That's not really what's worrying me."

Kane looked at her. "Go on."

"If this whole area is dark, then the reactor, or at least the part dedicated to both main and backup power, is out. To get to Delta, we might have to see what the problem is. Got much experience with compact reactors?"

"Zero."

"Ditto."

"Our PDAs should have a basic schematic. Maybe instructions for an emergency shutdown or restart."

Maria brought her PDA up, and in seconds she had cycled through a few menus before Kane could even look at his.

"Okay. There's something here. Shows a reactor control panel. Might help. No choice anyway."

"Great. Okay, lights on. And slowly. We don't want any surprises down here."

Kane would have insisted on taking the lead. But with Maria by his side, he knew better than to even suggest that.

Their steps echoed strangely in the dark corridor, as if the darkness itself made the sound carry farther, bouncing off the walls, the floor, the ceiling.

If anything was in there, Kane knew it would see and hear the two of them well before they could see it. He just had to hope that since they were traveling some back alleyway to Delta, it might be as deserted as it felt.

Funny thing about hope, he thought. Like a magic ability that can somehow keep you going.

Once, as they walked, he felt Maria's right hand, holding her machine gun, just graze his left hand, which clutched the shotgun. *The romance of weapons*, he thought. Still, that little bit of human contact felt good.

"You okay?" he asked, his voice a whisper. No sense in adding to whatever alert the noise they made was sending out.

"Yeah. I'm okay."

Their other hands each held one of the small

flashlights, with their second weapon slung over a shoulder. They performed a rhythmic scan, moving the twin pools of light from the front, then to the side, and on up to the ceiling, over their heads, and down the other side.

Until their small beams came back to the starting position, facing directly ahead, and they started the pattern again. Their steps were slow so as not to outpace the scan of their lights. And so far the only thing they had seen was the smooth polished metal of the walls, ceiling, and floor. Ahead, though, Kane saw that they were slowly coming to an intersection.

He leaned toward Maria and whispered: "Do we go that way or—?"

She shook here head, and also kept her voice down. "No. We go straight. That's another path to the new comm unit. There should even be a view of the outside from there, if I remember correctly."

The outside . . . What time was it? Day, night? Did it matter?

"So we just go straight?"

Another nod from Maria.

They came to the intersection, and walked even more slowly as they neared it, almost creeping up to it. It would be a perfect spot for a surprise.

Kane edged out ahead of Maria and took the first look.

The corridor in either direction looked empty. But

at the far end of the right corridor, he could see an observation area, probably for a visual inspection of the satellite towers.

The window was dark. Martian night. A faint glow at the line where the rocky landscape met the sky. The stars visible so brilliantly in the thin atmosphere of Mars. But he only permitted himself the slightest glance before quickly snapping to scan the front, the long corridor stretching ahead of them.

"At the end, there should be—according to my PDA—an entrance to the Delta Reactor Systems Control," Maria said. "Used to be filled with workers." Her voice was barely audible.

"So where are they all gone?"

"Good question." She took a breath. "I'm afraid we might get the answer."

Kane flexed his fingers. They took a few more steps.

Kane tapped Maria's shoulder. "Slowly now . . ."

He didn't like the way the narrow corridor they were in, almost a tube, opened up into something larger, something unseen. He couldn't see the dimensions and shape of that room. It appeared dimly lit ahead, but way too dim.

He sensed Maria looking at him. "Keep your light on," he said.

His own small tungsten lamp sent out a sharp spear of intense white light.

"What's up, Kane? You know something you want to share?"

He looked at her, and he realized why his every nerve ending felt electric. He had walked through the complex; he'd been cornered, attacked, trapped, and nearly killed. Instinct was taking over.

He pointed to the path ahead. "This the only way to go?"

"Yes, unless you want to backtrack to the monorail. But I wouldn't recommend—"

He held up his PDA. "And why does the schematic show nothing about the big space ahead?"

"We're backing up to Delta. Neither your nor my clearance gets us that. Technically, we shouldn't even be here."

"So we're close?"

"I didn't say that. Just that whatever is behind the walls to our right is all Delta. Off-limits."

"And the rear entryway?"

"Also off-limits. But I assume we're not going to worry about that, right?"

Kane nodded. "Okay. So we go forward without knowing what's ahead. Lights on—the light in the room ahead looks like it might give out any second."

A click, and Maria shined her light up at her face.

"Starting to sound a lot like a lieutenant again, Kane."

He smiled. Then: "Yeah, guess I am."

They turned back to the corridor, to the open area just ahead, and with their lights cutting arcs back and forth, they were on the move again.

30

MARIA WALKED SHOULDER TO SHOULDER with Kane. Despite her jokes, his words had rattled her. She trusted his instinct, and her fingers were now a claw wrapped around the trigger of her gun.

Only a few steps, and they'd enter the large open area, next to the walls of the off-limits Delta Lab. Her flashlight caught what seemed to be dust floating in the air, like a musty attic just opened, the motes caught by the white lights, swirling and dancing in anticipation of their entry.

In between each step they took, she tried to listen for some noise that would indicate that something lay ahead. There was a distant, constant hum—some machine—but nothing else.

One more step and they'd be in the large open area. They took it together, crossing some magical threshold that would finally allow them to aim those lights up and look around.

"Oh, God," Maria whispered.

Both her hands were full, but she wanted to grab Kane's arm, hold it for dear life. "No," she moaned.

Now her light moved along the walls slowly as she tried to take it all in, understand what they were seeing. At first glance, it looked as though the walls and ceiling themselves had melted as if made out of candle wax—melted, and then hardened in a flash.

But it was what was embedded in the "wax" that she made sense of only gradually, like an optical illusion. There were recognizable shapes: arms, legs, a bit of a head, an open mouth, the curve of a shoulder sticking out.

The walls and ceiling were covered with bodies.

"Are they all dead?" she asked.

Kane's light had stopped on one bulging shape—a head. Eyes wide open, mouth a small cavern, arms either missing or twisted backward into a shape that would have rendered them broken and useless.

"I'd say dead. Guess we could nudge one and see what happens."

"Right," Maria said. "You first. What did this to them?"

"Not sure I want to know the answer to that question."

"Let's keep walking."

They brought their lights down and aimed them forward. Maria truly hoped that each one stuck on the wall was dead—because she didn't know what she'd do if one suddenly stirred and came to life as she walked under it.

"Careful," Kane said. He pointed his light down at

the ground. Something wet, glistening, there. "Don't step in that, whatever it is."

"I've seen enough vids to know that," she said, moving slightly to the left, away from Kane, as they both dodged the strange puddle and whatever had produced the leak above them.

Maria resisted the temptation to aim her light up and look.

The puddle continued, and Maria just wanted it to end so that they could walk through this cave in tandem. That would feel a whole lot better.

Then: a whistling noise, the pitch rising. Maria started to speak: "What the—"

A handgun, spinning through the air, smashed into her head and she went flying to the ground.

Her light rolled from her left hand, and she reached up to her forehead and felt blood. Kane knelt down to her. "Are you—"

And then what looked like the metal leg of a chair came flying through the air. She could see it, and yelled just as it was about to hit Kane. But that split second of warning was enough for Kane to dodge the worst of it. Still, the flying metal bar grazed his head and sent him staggering to the right, nearly into the wall of bodies.

Maria knew that she had only seconds to act, to get back up and find out what was attacking them and stop it.

She rolled onto her knees as what was the rest of the chair smashed down into the space where she had been reclining. Again, mere seconds separated her from a blow that would have killed her.

She wanted her light, but that would have taken precious seconds away from her next moves: getting the machine gun, aiming it forward, while her left hand ripped one of the grenades from her belt.

"You okay?" Kane yelled.

But before she could answer, a high-pitched wailing noise filled the space, a sound that brought tears to her eyes. Then a loud *clack-clack*ing by something on the floor, and Maria waited until whatever was making the sound was finally caught by Kane's light.

And the horror before her made her gag. She registered its form even as her finger pulled tight.

Like some prehistoric crustacean, or heavily armored spider—only grown to the size of a room. Its legs sliced at the air as they hurried to bring the thing closer.

Maria noticed her bullets ricocheting off those legs, perfectly uselessly.

But atop the carapace, a near-human torso, save for the head with its multiple eyes and the mouth-like opening that issued its shrieking scream like a weapon.

Maria backed up. A quick glance to Kane to see him doing the same. Both had moved into the puddle now, and somewhere the still rational part of Maria's brain realized why it was wet.

This was the spot where it trapped any who came

this way. That was why it was fresh, wet, glistening—

The chair leg rose from the ground before the thing. It began a batonlike twirl, and then started whizzing toward her. Maria leaned right, and the chair leg went careening crazily past her.

A blast, then another. Kane firing his shotgun. And Maria saw a chunk of the thing's upper torso blow away. But it only seemed to make it scurry closer to them.

Then she remembered what she held in her left hand. A simple thumb movement released the safety and started the timer. More blasts from Kane, closer to the thing's head this time. One of its pincer legs reared up and then—like some old-fashioned telescope expanding—it uncurled and took a cutting swipe at Kane.

That's it, she thought. *Keep looking at him*. She rolled the grenade gently under the thing, not wanting to catch its attention. The spider creature had resurrected the chair and now sent it flying to Kane's left. When he dodged it, he'd have to move close enough for that pincer to skewer him.

The grenade rolled, and for a second Maria thought it would hit a leg and bounce back, useless. But it went neatly between two of the stamping pincers, under the thing's body.

Kane dodged the chair and fell into the wall. A front pincer started up.

And then the grenade exploded.

The explosion echoed weirdly in the room. Maria dug out a second grenade, thinking, *If one didn't stop it, then what the hell will another do?*

But the explosion blew away some of the legs; one leg came rolling to a stop right before her feet. And the body seemed to split in two as the torso looked down and around as if it something mysterious had suddenly gone wrong.

The spiderlike thing had obviously lost interest in its attack on Kane. But Kane was now close enough to put his shotgun to good use. When the head of the thing looked up after its damage inspection, Kane fired two rounds right at the head, biting off great chunks as if it were some kind of dense fruit.

The torso began a spastic waving and shaking, until—finally—it was motionless.

31

AXELLE—HER HELMET OFF—KEPT SUCKING in the tunnel air as if to prove to herself that it was in fact breathable. She detected a smell in the air—something metallic and sour—that made her gag.

But she could breathe it. She was alive, and—

She looked up at the cavern she had just entered, which kept growing wider and wider, so much so that her training in planetary geology told her that such an unsupported opening was—quite frankly—impossible.

And with every step she could see that the walls—all deeply lined with arabesque-like swirls merging into angular grooves and carvings—were beginning to glow even more.

She licked her lips. The taste of the air was even more vile than the smell.

She could see the walls glistening with a sheen of moisture. She stopped and looked back where she had come from, the path looking like an endless, ever narrowing umbilical leading back to what used to be Mars Excavation Site 3.

Not any longer. Axelle Graulich, lone survivor of the Martian Excavation Team, may have started in an excavation site, but this was someplace else.

Am I still on Mars? she wondered.

Another lick of her lips. She was thirsty, and even though she knew she had air to breathe here, how long before thirst started taking its toll on her. She picked up her PDA. No signal, of course. Nothing but the archived images and maps and information. The thing was useless here.

Still standing, she had the thought that somehow something was waiting for her at whatever the other end of this might be.

OUTSIDE DELTA LAB

Theo heard noises all around him. Screams, human screams, he thought. A terrible howling followed by silence as it ended. Until another screaming voice filled the halls here. And gunshots! So many sounds of bullets and explosions, until they too went quiet.

He mouthed a word, being careful not to say it. He just made the shape with his mouth, a silent puff of air. . . .

Please . . .

And even though he had been so quiet, just

standing there against a wall with bright light, he heard sounds. Steps.

Help is coming, he thought.

But it took only a moment to see how wrong he was.

INSIDE DELTA

MacDonald pressed the keys on his PDA, feverishly getting down everything that he thought he now knew. He understood what had happened. Yes, it was now all so clear. And even though he was curled up behind an overturned lab table, hiding and unable to dictate into the PDA, he could still write.

And then . . . and then, when a radio signal came back, he could send the message, and let the world know what was really happening here.

And what could happen everywhere . . .

He paused for a second and tugged at his crotch. Hours ago he had urinated, when the mad parade of things streamed out of the portal, and MacDonald, unable to move, could just barely see them as they emerged to begin their conquest of Mars City.

Because that's what it was like. He wrote that. An army. Conquest, and an ancient war begun again. . . .

And maybe he alone understood what could be done, what might be done to stop this. If it wasn't already too late. If it wasn't already completely hopeless.

The gunfire had subsided from outside Delta Lab. The marines there now were all dead or transformed.

No, he wrote. *Recruited.* There was something about the human creatures turning into zombies that seemed voluntary. Did they have to . . . some way, somehow . . . *want* to become part of this army of horrors?

So many questions, but he kept tapping the keys, knowing that he might not have much more time to get it all down.

His fingers danced over the tiny keyboard.

Word after word, until:

"Dr. MacDonald. So good of you to remain here. With us."

And MacDonald looked up to the master in charge of the Delta Labs—Dr. Malcolm Betruger, standing right over him.

BALLARD DEEP OCEAN RESEARCH LAB

David listened as Julie explained her observations to one of the new arrivals, Dr. Ati Watanabe.

"We've recorded the process, and it's been replicated each time. No doubt in my mind. . . ."

Watanabe looked at Julie more than at the 3-D loops on the screen, which showed the bacteria taking command of the tube worm host. Julie's strong point never was dealing with peers. Watanabe seemed to be evaluating Julie.

"What she means, Dr. Watanabe—" David started to say, to present Julie's point a bit more politically.

But Julie fired a look at him that said *Back off*, and she continued.

"Look, I've already uploaded the core data to the main server, which you and your team have full clearance to. I have my theories, of course, but maybe you, your team—with the help of Dr. Krasanov—could start taking a look."

David spotted Watanabe smile. Maybe Julie's reputation had preceded her.

"Yes. Thank you for all your preliminary work, Dr. Chao."

Touché, thought David.

"My team will begin examining the data immediately. I've already spoken to Dr. Krasanov. Perhaps you would be interested in joining the team? I am sure once we begin examining the nanogenetics of the symbiotic process, we will have our hands full."

For a second David thought Julie would tell Dr. Watanabe what he could do with his offer of collaboration. But instead she took a breath and smiled.

"I'd be honored."

"Great," David said. "Then I will leave you to it. I have another sub arriving within the hour—not sure where I'm going to put everyone."

David started to walk away, but Julie ran up to him and grabbed his elbow.

"Proud of me?" she asked quietly.

"Hmmm?"

"Wasn't I polite with Dr. W.?"

"Very." Then David smiled. "Thanks for that."

"This is too important, isn't it, David? For ego. For any of that."

"Absolutely. I better—"

But she had one more thing to say. "Do you think any of this will make a difference?"

What a question, David thought. They had seen the vids, the creatures, the terror, the mayhem taking place a world away. Could whatever they do down here have any impact, any meaning? He doubted it.

Instead of saying that, he said, "I hope so. And I'm going to run this place like everything we do counts and the clock is ticking."

Julie gave his arm another gentle squeeze. "Good."

And she turned and walked away as David hurried to the sub bay, and the next batch of the UAC's finest scientists.

UAC HEADQUARTERS

Ian Kelliher would have liked nothing more than a few fingers of scotch. He would have liked to feel that hit, and let some of the roiling emotions and fears that held him tight, like a hand squeezing, all fade away.

He knew that was out of the question. *There will be time for that after this ends.* If *this ends,* he thought.

He had all three screens in his office up and on, all showing images from the UAC subterranean lab.

"Karla, don't let anything interrupt me, unless you hear directly from Hayden or Campbell on Mars. I assume we're still getting nothing from there?"

"Yes, sir. Still quiet. Mr. Kelliher, no interruption even for a message from Captain Hakala, sir? He's due to check in with you in the next half hour."

"No. No one else. I will let you know when you can let any contacts through."

"Yes, sir."

Then Kelliher shut off the voice link to his assistant. Now she would be cut off until he wanted to speak to her again. At the same time, Kelliher hit a button on his desk, and he could hear through an earpiece the sounds from the lab deep below the headquarters building. His chief there, Dr. Adoni, raced between the two portals, mirror images of the portals found on Mars.

"Silvio, how do things progress?"

The scientist stopped in his tracks and put a finger up to his earpiece.

"Fine, sir. I think we are ready. I have my team recording everything; we even injected some micro-monitors into the subject's bloodstream to measure blood flow, cellular response, and——"

"Very good, Doctor. Can you begin?"

Kelliher could see that the man wasn't too pleased. Kelliher knew that Adoni had long viewed the live experiments on Mars as great risks, even with animal subjects. Now they had led to an out-break on Mars that no one understood at all. And yet they were about to do the same thing here.

Kelliher knew it was risky. But he had no choice. All of Mars, all the investments, the plans, the hopes for a different future for humanity, could vanish. Replaced with—what?—a siege from somewhere unknown.

No choice, Kelliher told himself. He must do whatever he could to find out what happened, to stop it. The risk was immense. But so was the danger of doing nothing.

He took a breath.

"Then, Silvio, if all is ready. Let's do this. . . ."

32

MARS CITY

JACK CAMPBELL HAD PRACTICED WITH THE BFG-9000 only one time, at the Colorado base that was home to the Mars transports. The gun could be tricky to get into firing position, he knew. The weight, and the momentum of all that weight, meant one had to move slowly.

And due to its massive firepower, the safety system involved a three-step process to ready the gun for actual firing. The auto ammo loader had to be engaged, and then the basic trigger release thrown. But then finally the targeting display, which could— if the shooter wanted—lock on a target's unique heat signature, had to be manually engaged.

Then there was the matter of balance. The thing was heavy from end to end, and only if one had a lot of muscle strength could it be held in position while firing. Not a gun for underachievers, Campbell had thought as he used it to blow up target buildings and vehicles on the aboveground range in Colorado. No point in issuing a lot of the oversized guns, since how many people could operate them?

He could, though. And whatever lay ahead was about to find that out as well.

Campbell walked past the marines in Reception, all simply standing around. They looked like they were waiting for doom to arrive.

"Look lively," he barked to the room. "Who the hell's in charge here?"

A private came forward.

Did any officers survive the shock waves? Campbell wondered.

"I'm McCullough. A guy named Kane told me to keep things . . . under control."

Kane. So that bastard was still alive. Not surprising. A lot of grunts and private contractors like Campbell admired what Kane did to save his troops. Of course, he got shafted for that. In the corps, an order is an order.

"Okay, McCullough. But these other guys, they look like they're ready to collapse from boredom. Get them to check perimeters. Goddamn it—you don't want something creeping up on you, right?"

McCullough grinned. "You got that right. Hey, are you military?"

Campbell shook his head. "Back in the day. Once. Now just a private contractor for the UAC."

He noticed McCullough eyeing the gun.

"Got any more of"—he pointed at the BFG—"those?"

Now Campbell grinned. "I wish. Just got this—"

And then the earpiece in both men's ears belched out static, followed by voices. They stood there and listened, their eyes on each other. The radio was up again. And now they could at last hear the horror, loud and clear.

Kane 's earpiece came to life, and he saw Maria turn at the same moment. Except—instead of one voice—it seemed as if a dozen different radio streams were competing for the same bandwidth.

"Hold on," Kane said. "We should listen."

They stood there, close to Delta now, and listened. . . .

"They're gone, shit—all wiped out. Is anyone there, God, is anyone the hell hearing this . . . ?"

It jumped to another voice.

". . . stopped here. Both ends, but we're bottled up, man. Reinforcements urgently . . ."

Another skip, another voice. Female this time, calm and cool.

". . . any unit getting this—you must reset your frequencies. Repeat, reset . . ."

Then gone. And then another, once close.

". . . Kelly, he's leading them! Christ, he's actually helping them. You gotta come here, you gotta . . ."

"Should we—"

Kane held up a hand. This jumble of voices was giving him a picture of what surrounded them. It said that there were some space marines alive, still in place, still—technically—functional. But it also told him that more marines had joined the others—whatever hellish army now roamed Mars City.

Maria nodded. Another voice. Quiet, plaintive in its repetition . . .

"*. . . is Elliot Swann, personal representative of UAC head Ian Kelliher. I am by the comm station. If I don't hear from anyone, I will alert the Armada that an immediate evac is needed. Repeat, this is . . .*"

The signal faded. And then there was nothing.

"Radio dead?" Kane asked.

But Maria walked over to him and touched his earpiece. He heard a pinging noise.

"There. I just reset your radio. I guess when they came back online the system hadn't put them back in their various channels. So, now we have communication—that is, if there's anyone left to communicate with." She looked at him.

"Is there anyone we should talk to?"

Maria shook her head. "I think once we use our radios, then we're walking targets."

"Agreed. If we need to, we know they work. Let's keep going."

Swann . . .

Campbell stopped. If there was one thing Campbell knew, it was that calling for a rescue by the Armada was the completely wrong thing. If the big ships came, they might be able to take out a lot of the creatures.

But would those troops be affected, if this was an infection? Could there be any guarantees that it was safe?

No, Campbell thought. *This is our problem until it's solved.*

He touched his earpiece. It squeaked, and then he cycled to the last radio signature.

"Swann, it's Campbell."

"Jack! Jeezus, Jack—what's happening?"

"Look, things are getting . . . under control."

"What? Do you hear what everyone is saying? It's insanity here, Jack. I'm going to send the signal to the Armada. Hayden would want that."

"No, Swann. I just came from Hayden. His link to the Comm Center is still down, but he doesn't want anyone coming here. Not now, not yet."

Swann was a good counselor, Campbell guessed. But this took him way over his head. He could imagine Swann curled up at the far end of the complex, itching to bring down fresh squads of marines and be rescued. Those marines by now would have seen images of what they were to face, each one thinking: *I didn't sign on for* this.

"Look, Elliot, I—"

Then: movement at the far end. Two . . . three figures. Could be marines, Campbell thought, but not from the way they walked. One stepped into a pool of light, and Campbell could see that it *used* to be a marine. Even had a helmet on. Tattered uniform, a hook for an arm or maybe just a piece of bone that somehow kept growing. It also held a chain gun and was starting to aim.

"Hold on, Swann."

As good a time as any to test the BFG. The targeting display could cover all three of them, or it could be narrowed to hit each one with pinpoint accuracy. Since it fired a few rounds every second, Campbell opted for the latter.

The first blast blew the head off the first marine zombie. The other two started hurrying toward Campbell as best they could, each armed, one with a machine gun, another with what looked like a shotgun.

"Bye," Campbell said, and he filled their bodies with so many blasts that it sent them flying backward onto the ground, chewed into pieces.

"Quite a weapon . . ." Campbell said.

"What?" Swann said, still panicked. "What the hell just happened?"

"Nothing. Don't worry. I know where you are. I'll get there and we can decide what to do together. You got that, Swann? . . . Swann, do you goddamn *hear* me?"

"Yes."

"Don't do a thing. We'll see what's happening and act together. Just like Kelliher would want us to do. Got it?"

"Yes."

Campbell took a breath. He hoped that he had put a new fear into Swann's head—a fear that he would get his ass kicked if he did anything at the comm station.

"Great. And meanwhile, don't use your personal radio again until I contact you. Starting . . . now."

No answer. Which was good.

Campbell looked at his PDA. He was close to the Comm Center. He guessed there might be a bigger need for this gun at Delta, but for now getting Swann on board with the program outweighed that.

More lives would be lost. *This peach of day isn't over yet*, Campbell thought.

He started down the hallway, ready to march over the dead marines turned into a bloody mess.

2145

INTO HELL

33

HAYDEN STARTED LOOKING AT THE IMAGES coming on from all the marine units, many of them wiped out by now.

One of the creatures—what looked like a head mounted on legs, with a jaw that snapped at the legs of panicked soldiers—made his stomach tighten, ready to vomit.

Some of the images came with names supplied by the grunts fighting the . . .

These, for example, *ticks*. *Ticks from hell*, thought Hayden.

Then another image, something with two heads, vaguely human-looking even though it crawled on the ground, scurrying. Some grunt called it a maggot as he recorded its image. Belly up, its inside exploded by a grenade.

Hayden looked out the window. His assistant still sat at her desk. A half-dozen well-armed marines stood guard outside. And though it was a craven thought for a military man of Hayden's experience, he felt good knowing that he had a wall of that much firepower between him . . . and what was now roaming free through all of Mars City.

He had heard the exchange between Campbell and Swann too. And though he was tempted to tell Swann to ask the Aramda to land, he knew that could be the one thing that would transform this disaster into—what?—perhaps something that could end humanity.

I have to stay cool, Hayden told himself. *Too much at stake here. Can't panic. Must not panic.*

He moved to the next video. Seeing something that looked like a wall of flesh, and . . . tusks? Or what the hell were they? He saw the things hanging from the bulbous creature's head quickly wrap around the necks of two soldiers at once, instantly squeezing them to death.

It took six men to bring it down. What if there were an army of such things?

Stay calm, Hayden told himself. *Calm, cool,* he told himself, over and over.

"You knew about this?"

Kellyn MacDonald tried to not let his fear show, with Betruger towering over him.

The head scientist of Mars City laughed. "Of course. What do you think, MacDonald, that I couldn't see what was happening, where our experiments led?" He leaned down. "And how important they were? No, I'm afraid I knew *exactly* what we were doing."

"And the others?"

"Your . . . compatriots? A few I took into my confidence, but most had to be kept just like you. Shocked, concerned, confused—while the process went forward. Unfortunately, those others had to be sacrificed but they were good"—a smile filled Betruger's face—"coconspirators . . . for a while."

"What the hell have you done?"

Betruger tilted his head and arched his eyebrows. "How astute. What the . . . hell indeed, Dr. MacDonald. But I'm guessing that is a rhetorical question from you? You have"—Betruger gestured at the bloody slaughterhouse that was Delta—"seen all this happen. You've seen *them,* right. You're a smart man. You can guess what the 'hell' happened."

MacDonald shook his head. "You're completely insane."

"Really? Seems like I'm the one who will survive all this. And this, Mars, is only the beginning. And I will be there to see it all, to *participate.* . . ."

At that moment Betruger raised his left hand as if reaching for something bright and wonderful amid the smoky ruins of the lab. And MacDonald saw it was no longer a hand. Fingers still protruded out of what now resembled the large pincers of a crab. Betruger himself looked at it.

"Oh—interesting, hm? Trying it on. There will be other rewards too. Many other rewards . . ."

Betruger was actually relishing being turned into a monster. That was even more horrible than the transformation itself.

"You have the same planned for me."

It was a statement. But surprisingly Betruger shook his head. "Oh, no. I knew, of course, that you were here all the time. I could sense it. But it felt good to have you, one of my closest colleagues, observe all *this*. Now you have served that purpose. And—"

He clicked two ends of the claw together.

"—that purpose has come to an end. There is only one more purpose you can serve now. With all the dwindling numbers . . . not many like you left alive here, and so—"

Betruger reached down with his claw and grabbed MacDonald's left leg between the ankle and knee. Then, the pain excruciating, overwhelming, the claws closed. Over his own screams, MacDonald heard a *snap*.

"There, now for the other one."

The pain from the broken bone, the lower mangled leg, completely masked the same thing occurring to his right leg. He howled, his voice shrieking.

"Yes, scream away, Dr. MacDonald. Because, you see, soon from over there will come some new ones. Hungry. And you will be here, alive, waiting. Their first meal."

MacDonald flailed, shaking his head as if that would somehow stop the flow of words.

"And for now, I must of course join the others. Mars City is only our beginning. But our end—"

He started walking away . . . and kept talking without turning back.

"—our end will truly be something wondrous, amazing, eternal. Eternal, Dr. MacDonald. . . ."

"Hold on there, Counselor . . ."

Campbell entered the control room for the Comm Center. Everything looked perfectly normal, save for Elliot Swann sitting at a console.

Elliot Swann turned to Campbell.

"I—I have the Armada in contact, Jack. I could send a message right away."

Campbell took a step. He was tempted to simply blast the console and end all debate about summoning the Armada for a rescue. But even though he suspected that there was a backup system that could get online, he wanted to do this without rendering Mars City incommunicado.

"They're waiting, Jack. They could be here in hours. Get us the hell off here."

"Right, Swann. Get us off, and whatever else we might bring with us. Then what? Take us back to Earth? That sound good, Swann?"

Swann looked away as if he might be considering the repercussions of an Armada landing for the first time.

"Now tell me—does that sound like a good idea?"

Swann turned back to him, staring at the BFG-9000, which was pointed in his general direction. Not that Campbell planned on using it.

He saw Swann gulp. His eyes sunken. The man's fear almost something he could smell.

"Wh-what are we going to do, Jack? What the *hell* are we going to do?"

Campbell felt that Swann had at last pulled back from the precipice and was ready to listen. "We have to secure Mars City, Swann. We have to try and stop this—contain this—before we let anyone come here. You understand that, don't you?"

Swann nodded. True acceptance or merely some rote reflex? It was hard to tell.

"But who's left?"

"There are plenty of people left. Plenty," Campbell lied. "Whole squads back at Transport and Reception. Other teams are securing Alpha. But we have a real big problem."

Swann's dark eyes were locked on him.

"This all comes from Delta Lab. And that, well, that area is not secure. Something is still going on—"

Swann started shaking his head, "I don't think . . . God, I really, really don't think—"

Campbell pulled his right hand off the BFG and gave Swann a strong back slap. Swann's haunted eyes popped open wide.

"Listen, Swann, let me do the thinking, okay? You see, if we don't stop what's going on in Delta, then nobody will get out of here—or off Mars. Nobody." He paused to let the words sink in a bit. "So you have two choices. You can go back to Reception. A long trek. Might see some of the uglies along the way. In fact, you probably will. Or"—he tapped

the gun—"you can come with me. Me and my"—
Campbell grinned, using a line from a vid from over
a hundred years ago—"little friend. You do know
how to shoot, right?"

Swann nodded. Campbell guessed that Swann
wouldn't be much use in a firefight. But one way or
the other, he wanted the panicked lawyer away from
the Comm Center.

Campbell took a breath. "So what's it going to
be?"

Swann cleared his throat; then, as if he had been
glued to the contoured chair before the control
panel, he stood up.

"I'll go with you, Jack. You're right. We have to
stop it."

Campbell patted Swann on the back. "Good
man." He grabbed his PDA. "There's a spur of the
monorail near here. And it will take us right there.
Take this—" He handed Swann a machine gun.
"Safety's off, so be careful. All set?"

A nod, and then Campbell led the terrified Elliot
Swann out of the control room, thinking, *If the poor
bastard only knew how scared I am too, he wouldn't
move an inch.*

34

KANE STOPPED FIRING, BUT HE HEARD MARIA let off a few more blasts at the latest things to try and stop them.

In what was becoming standard procedure for them as they fought their way forward to Delta, they stood back-to-back to cover a 360-degree arc.

"Think they're dead enough?"

Maria shrugged. He imagined she was as exhausted as he was, but both of them resisted using more stims. Diminishing returns, Kane knew, and could lead to a collapse.

"So," Kane said, looking at the pile of bodies around them, "mind telling me where these zombies got chain saws from?"

"Sure, as long you tell me how the chain saws became part of their bodies."

"Guess it makes them easier to use."

"Seriously—under Delta there is a massive warehouse that's used by the excavation teams. Looks like these former grunts went in there, maybe running from the blast, and this is what happened."

They stood there for a second, and the moment of giddiness at being alive began to fade. "The key thing," Kane said, "is that these things can just—I dunno—affix things to their bodies."

"That's insane."

"Yeah, but if it's true, if it's what you might call a 'rule,' then we got to be prepared for anything."

Only now did she turn and look at him. "I thought I was."

He laughed, the sound so human, so good. "Guess you are."

They had activated the Delta reactor, restarting the main and backup controls. The place would be powered. The chain-saw zombies had been a momentary distraction.

"Okay, guess we're ready, then. And Delta?" he asked.

She turned and pointed to a door at the end of the room, across the sea of dead chainsaw zombies. "There. It's an observation room, and my PDA shows direct access to the lab."

Kane nodded and together, taking care as they moved, they headed to the last barrier before entering the rear section of Delta Labs.

"Goddamn," Kane said. "Door is locked. What do we—"

But when he turned around he saw Maria picking through some of the dead corpses.

"What are you doing?"

She turned, her face all scrunched up, and waved

a PDA at him. "I'm guessing that one of these things had the right security clearance."

"Good thinking."

She brought the PDA up to the security lock. "Okay—here goes."

Kane waited. The lock glowed red, then turned to green. "Open sesame."

"Once we walk in," Maria said, "we'll technically be in Delta. At least that's what the schematics show."

He grabbed the handle and pulled the door open. . . .

The room was empty; still, they kept their guns leveled, ready. "Everyone moved on?" Kane said.

"Guess so."

They walked through the small room, a lab of some kind. Half the ceiling lights were damaged, but there was enough of a milky glow to see this small lab—and something standing in the center of the room.

Kane walked up to it.

TELEPORTER STATION 5, it said.

"Teleportation. Is that what they were doing? Do you think—"

But Maria had walked to the far wall, and stood at a glass window. "Kane, come and look at this."

He walked up to her, and he could see what was obviously the main Delta Lab. A massive room, with at least three more of the teleporter stations. Bodies all over. But no creatures. At least, not yet.

One of the teleporters looked on fire, a liquid fiery glow filling it, shifting, fluttering as if caught in some unknown breeze; it lit the room with a brilliant yellow-red glow.

"What is that?" Maria said.

"Not sure we want to know. But we have to get in there." Kane looked left and right, but he could see no doors, no potential entrance.

"There's got to be a way."

Maria also started to look around, but the empty smaller lab only led out. If there was a way between this room—an observation station of some kind—into the other room, it wasn't clear.

"I don't see anything," she said.

"Me either. Does that mean we have to go back and—"

"*Help* . . ." The sound was a croak, almost not human. But Kane couldn't imagine any of the creatures asking for such a human thing as help.

"You heard that?" he said to Maria.

She nodded. "I'm trying to locate it. Not sure—"

"*Please* . . ."

She turned back to the observation window and tapped it.

"There! It's coming from inside there."

Kane came and stood beside her as they scanned the room. Until—

"God, I see him." She said. "Poor bastard. Over by that table."

Kane spotted a man sprawled on the ground by

an overturned lab table. He could also see that something had been done to his lower legs.

Kane raised a hand to the man, who acknowledged the move with the slightest tilt of his head. The room's intercoms still worked.

"Is there a way into the lab from here?"

The man cleared his throat, a low gravelly sound as he struggled to talk. "Yes. There is. Y-you . . . need to come quickly. There's no . . . time."

Kane answered: "What do we do?"

The man pointed to one of the teleportation pods standing quiet. Then his finger pointed, just past Kane, to the pod in the observation room.

"You have to use . . . the teleporter. Use it . . . to come here."

Maria answered quickly. "No. That can't be safe."

"Listen . . ." the man said, struggling to get the words out. "It is safe for short distances. We—we tested it with humans. It was safe . . . up to a point."

"Kane, I don't like it."

"You can use it to get in here. That short distance . . . always seemed safe."

Maria came closer to Kane. "Come on—we'll go the other way in."

Kane looked at her. "You see that." He pointed to the other pod, the one that glowed like an open wound of color and heat. "My guess is that has to be stopped. And we sure as hell can't do it here."

The scratchy voice from within Delta: "You have to hurry."

"Right."

Kane walked over to the teleporter and looked at the controls. "I'll go through, and you go find another way into Delta."

"This is crazy." Then, to the man in the other room. "Talk me through how to use this."

The man coughed, and then slowly began to explain how to use the device that would transport Kane into the other room.

Kane pressed a button. The screen in front of him flashed: TELEPORTATION SEQUENCE INITIATED.

Then: TRANSMISSION IN 60 SECONDS.

A timer counted down as Kane stepped into the chamber. He smiled at Maria. "Meet me on the other side. When you can. Maybe I'll have the whole thing shut down by the time you get there."

"I don't like this."

A matching screen told Kane he had thirty seconds. "Tell you the truth, neither do I. But not much choice."

He put a hand to the thick clear hull of the pod. "Just wish me luck."

Maria raised a hand to the pod shell, matching Kane's, and shook her head. "Good luck, Kane."

And then the chamber filled with a brilliant white cloud, followed by thin spears of electricity that erupted from the center of the chamber.

Maria had closed her eyes. And when she opened them, Kane was gone.

35

KANE HAD CLOSED HIS EYES TOO. *After all*, he thought, *if I'm going to be transformed into a zombie, maybe with bits of my weapons attached to my body, I'd rather not watch it happen.*

But when he opened his eyes, everything *looked* to be in the right place, and outside of a slight ringing in his ears, he didn't feel any different. *Did it not work?* he thought for a second. But looking up, he saw that he was in Delta, and he saw the other chamber, the swirling vortex of yellow and red, close by.

He opened the chamber door and stepped out, hurrying to the man on the ground.

"Okay, what can you tell me about what's happening here?"

The man's eyes looked at Kane's. "I will. I—I'll tell you everything you need. But when I'm done . . . I want you to hand me your gun."

Kane looked at the man's legs. The bottoms twisted into complete uselessness.

"Agreed?" the man insisted.

"Agreed."

The man looked at the fiery chamber. "My name is Dr. Kellyn MacDonald. The experiments done here opened a portal to . . . someplace else. That"—his finger pointed at the molten swirl—"is the opening. Things have come from there, and those who have been touched by it . . . become changed. But"—MacDonald's eyes drifted back to Kane—"you have seen them."

"Yes. And I want to stop it. I need to shut it down. Can you tell me what to do, how to—"

The man nodded. He raised his other hand, and Kane saw that the scientist had his fingers tightly wrapped around a PDA. "It's in . . . here. All you need. Read it. Then—"

His eyes went wide as the man's head exploded as a shell of some kind hit it. Kane rolled to his right.

So stupid, he thought. *Letting my guard down. So damn stupid.*

As he rolled, he tried to get his shotgun into position. But he could hear blasts tracing a path toward him. He caught a glimpse of what was shooting at him.

A living skeleton, covered with skin—and with what looked like twin cannons or small rocket launchers perched on its shoulders, shooting at Kane.

No—not *on* the thing's shoulders, but part of them.

Kane raised his shotgun, but the thing was easily a few seconds ahead of him, taking a step that made its leathery skin ripple. Kane might get off a volley, but he was about to be blown to bits.

Which was when the thing's head erupted after a concentrated blast of a dozen machine gun bullets hit it, passing through the skull and out the other side.

The skeleton demon stood there a moment as if pondering what just happened. Then it collapsed, falling full-length before the prone Kane.

"Moraetes," he whispered.

"I figured if it was okay for you"—she nodded in the direction of the teleporter—"then it's good enough for me."

"I didn't see that thing appear."

"It came from there."

"Yeah. It's a portal. To God knows where."

"It came out just as I finished beaming over."

"Feel okay?"

She smiled. "I think so. And you?"

"Yeah." Now he turned back to MacDonald. "We were too late to save this guy, but—" Kane got up and walked to the dead scientist. He leaned down and removed the PDA from the man's death clutch. "—but maybe he can save us all."

He hit the PDA, and the screen came to life, the last entry already on the screen. Maria walked over.

And they read the last entry of Dr. Kellyn Mac-Donald together.

Mars City PDA
Dr. Kellyn MacDonald
Personal Folder, Security Enabled.
Checked and Opened_03_13_2145 18:23:10

I don't know how much time I have. I expect I will be dead soon, and the only hope for telling what I know—what I believe—will be this document. If it's not found, it could all be lost. Humankind itself might be lost.

Know this: the things that now roam Mars City come from a universe away, a place as real as our universe but a place of nightmares and horror. I have seen them emerge, crawling out from the portal that Betruger's experiments created, eager to feed off the life they find here, and eager to reach beyond Mars City.

If they were to gain an opening to Earth, then it would surely all be hopeless. And I have seen what no one else has: how the creatures come out and are shaped. As if they can sense our fantasies, the terrors, the images that have haunted us since we first huddled in caves—and they *become* those horrors. Our own imagination becomes our worst enemy, used by these beings. Is there a limit to what they can become? I have not seen any such limit.

And now the material found at Site 3 all becomes clear. How the great Martian civilization faced extinction—complete and hopeless—when somehow they opened a portal to that universe. They could not save themselves. But they could stop it. They created something that could rival the power of the evil that threatened to possess this universe, the evil ready to turn Mars into a world of death and horror and destruction.

We called it U1. The artifact that was discovered at Site 3, something that Betruger started calling the Soul Cube, is a remnant of the long-ago civilization. Except it wasn't merely a dead artifact from that lost civilization. The true souls, the opposing force of their existence, became channeled into this device, making a weapon which could finally rival in power the terror from beyond.

But now this Soul Cube—that dam against the wave of madness—is gone, taken into the portal, taken into the other universe so that the beings here are free.

Time. There is no more time. It may already be too late, but if you read this, know one thing: only if you are armed with that ancient weapon can you truly stop them and close the portal. Without it, then the battle is truly finished.

And if you get back to Earth, please, please tell my family that my last thoughts were of them; and

Folder Closed and Locked_03_13_2145 18:23:10

Maria spun around.

"What?" Kane said.

"Thought I heard something back there. Something moving."

They both stood still, looking around the lab. At any minute they knew something else could emerge from the portal.

"At least we know what to do."

She looked up at him. "You do? And what the hell is that?"

Kane stared at the swirling maelstrom that was the gateway to another world. "I have to go in there. Get this Soul Cube. Use it—somehow. Stop this."

Maria looked like she was about to argue with him, but then they both heard a sound, and their weapons flew into position. Kane spotted something scurrying between tables, navigating the maze that was the destroyed lab.

"Hey!"

Maria looked at him, perhaps wondering why he didn't shoot.

"Come out."

And then she saw the small head pop up over the edge of the table.

36

MARIA WATCHED THE SMALL BOY COME OUT from behind the table.

"It's okay, son. You remember me?" Kane said.

"You know him?"

Kane took a step toward the boy and then crouched down. Maria saw him smile at the kid. "You scared, son? What's your name?"

The boy looked around the room. Maria had to wonder how much the boy had seen. His eyes looked haunted. Kane put out a hand and gave the boy's hair a gentle tousle. She thought he'd recoil at the touch, but he stood there.

"Theo."

"Theo." Kane looked at Maria. "I guess, Theo, you've been running around a lot. Hm? Seen a lot of things?"

The boy nodded, and Maria could see that the boy was on the edge, so close to crying. Crying, perhaps screaming.

"Well, we're going to get you out of here, Theo.

Back to where there are people. Lots of people." Another glance at Maria.

"Wait a minute, Kane. What are you saying?"

Kane continued to crouch close to the boy. "You can take Theo back. While I—"

The boy's eyes went wide. If he had been about to cry, he now let out a scream instead.

The portal had been quiet. But suddenly, things got busy.

Three zombies, guns molded to their twisted torsos, had stepped into the room. Then something leaped into the room, towering over the zombies. The thing's helmet-shaped head had eyes that darted left and right, taking in whatever was alive in the room. It made hissing noises that somehow the once-human zombies understood.

Kane pulled Maria and Theo back to the wall, the three of them pressing tight against the far end of Delta.

"Should we shoot?"

"No. They haven't seen us—yet."

Two other things crawled out of the portal, legs and arms acting like the appendages of a crab, twin heads, snapping left and right, now answering the hisses and groans of the tall creature that seemed to be directing them.

And then the zombies turned in a line and started heading to where Maria stood with Kane and the boy. The crawling things also scurried, one left, one right.

They were surrounded, and Maria knew there was no way they could survive the attack. The tall creature howled, and its squad of monsters started the attack.

"Now we shoot—" Kane said. Then: "Stay behind me, Theo."

Side by side, Maria and Kane fired, shotgun blasts merging with machine guns. Too-close quarters and too much movement to use the grenades. But all the shells were not nearly strong enough, the volleys not nearly enough.

In seconds it would be all over.

A cannonlike firing filled the room, the blasts immense, a sound Maria couldn't identify.

She turned to see two people—men who had come off the transport. And one of them held the biggest damn gun that Maria had ever seen.

She kept firing, but it seemed ineffectual compared to the display of firepower from the massive gun as it literally blew off chunks of the creatures. The tall creature tried to direct its now-beleaguered force to focus their attack on the newcomer.

But it was too late, as the cross fire from Maria and Kane added to the damage inflicted.

It was such an amazing sight, she almost felt like grinning.

Finally, the guy with the big gun targeted the commander of this legion from hell and fed a steady stream of rocket projectiles into the thing's open, howling maw.

Until the room filled with the smoke of gunpowder and the stench of the things bleeding out on the lab floor. And the skirmish was over.

Then the man with the mighty big fucking gun approached them.

His name was Campbell, the UAC security guy sent up here by Kelliher. And the other man—so scared that he could barely stand—was the lawyer. Could be a lot of lawsuits coming out of this mess.

Kane was finishing briefing them on what MacDonald's PDA told him had to be done.

"So, someone has to go in there?"

Kane nodded. "Yeah. Me."

For a moment the two men were eyeball to eyeball. "Maybe I should," Campbell said. "And bring this."

"I'm not sure any weapons will make it through— Christ, I don't know if I will. But I didn't come this far to have someone else finish the job."

"Then why not both of us?"

Kane took a breath. "I'm not sure I'll live walking into this thing. Not sure if any of these"—he held up his two guns—"will get through. And if I don't make it, that will leave *you*. Still here, alive with that"—he pointed at the BFG—"to do something."

Campbell smiled. "Tell you one thing, Lieutenant . . ."

Lieutenant. Been a while since he heard that. . . .

". . . you've got balls."

Kane grinned. "Or maybe I'm just stupid."

Maria shook her head. "You do take risks. . . ."

Kane turned to her. He was ready to argue with her again, but he could see Maria had her hand on Theo's shoulder, the boy practically melted into her. *Okay,* he thought, *she knows what to do.*

"C-can I go with them?" Swann asked, moving closer to Maria.

Campbell laughed. "No, Counselor. You stay right here with me. It's a big gun here, but I wouldn't mind another. *Capisce*?"

Kane turned and looked at the portal. He brought MacDonald's PDA up to his face and looked at the image of the Soul Cube. "If there's a way to bring this back . . . I will."

"And I'll be here making sure nothing is waiting for you when you come out."

Kane took a breath. "Sounds like a plan. Maria, I'll see you back at Reception."

"You better."

He would have liked to give her a hug, maybe another kiss. But that moment had moved on. It was time for him to enter the portal.

Kane turned away from them. "Best everyone stand back. Not sure what effect my entering may have."

"Good luck, Kane," Campbell said.

He hesitated a moment. The glowing swirl before him looked as if it could consume him. All this might be over for him in a matter of seconds. He waded into the center of the vortex, each step feeling leaden. His heart raced, and as his breathing became faster, he smelled the stench coming from the portal, a smell unlike anything he had ever experienced, even after so many years of fighting and bloodshed.

He didn't let his pace slacken. He hadn't, of course, admitted to them how scared he was. Perhaps the most frightening moment of his life.

Step after step, until there remained only one more step, into the swirling pool of fiery red and yellow.

He put his boot into the lower end of that swirl, and then he allowed his forward momentum to carry him forward.

Kane was immediately sucked into it with a violent vacuumlike gasp that pulled him from Mars, from this solar system, from this very universe. . . .

37

MARIA WATCHED KANE VANISH AND THEN SHE looked at Campbell, who—she could see—obviously knew better than to say any false words of encouragement. "Okay. . . ." She gave Theo's shoulder a squeeze. "Guess we're ready to go, hm?" She looked down at him. Theo didn't nod, didn't do anything, just stood there, glued to her side.

"Got your weapons all set? Ammo good?" Campbell asked.

"Fully loaded," she said. "You guys . . . do what you can to make sure that Kane gets out of there alive, okay?"

"You got it."

A last nod, then Maria started out of Delta, holding Theo close.

The force of entering the portal sent Kane flying into what felt at first like empty space. An intense nausea attacked his gut, and he coughed and hacked as his body spun, spitting out remnants of the water he had been drinking.

Instinctively, his hands went to his eyes to protect them from the blinding light. But that left his ears unprotected, and the roaring sound here—wherever "here" was—was similar to the noise that filled Mars City during each of the outbreaks, but louder, more piercing, causing horrible pain to his ears.

What was happening?

There was nothing solid around him, just the light, the noise, the smell, his own wrenching heaving into the air. But then Kane felt himself accelerating, and suddenly the sound lessened, and the smoky swirl of light gave way to something ahead as he was thrown onto hard ground, his hands falling from his eyes, his head smacking hard against the ground.

He was here. The other place.

I'm in hell, Kane thought. *Sweet God . . . I'm in hell.*

For a moment Kane stayed prone, looking at the world before him with his now-uncovered eyes.

The walls themselves glistened more like skin than stone. His hands, pressed tight against the ground, felt some give, as if that "rock" too was actually something else. The smell that had him retching so badly now completely filled this place. And though the roaring noise had subsided, a mix of screams and howling came from everywhere.

He got to his knees, looking for his weapons. Had they somehow been destroyed? But he looked left and saw a pile of weapons . . . as though everyone else who'd been here had also had them ripped away.

Kane got to his feet and grabbed his shotgun and machine gun, as well as the belt with his remaining grenades. At least he was armed.

Then a single high-pitched shriek *filled* this area, and the smaller spider-things—the trites—jumped on him, four, five of them, covering him, digging into his flesh. Two had locked on his arms, the legs closing viselike, making it impossible to aim his guns.

One of the trites crawled up his side, and now came close to Kane's head and neck.

So it ends like this, he thought. *A few seconds in hell, and then the bold brave attempt ends.*

No way.

He flung himself against one of the walls, feeling the skinlike texture but also making two of the trites squeal with the pressure. His left arm suddenly came free, his hand tight on the gun stock, finger on the trigger.

Had to do this carefully, to make sure he didn't end up blowing pieces of himself into the air. The first blast sent chunks of the creatures' flesh spraying all over Kane's face.

He heard their squeals—perhaps they knew that they had lost the initiative. If there wasn't one of the big spider creatures around, he might just survive this.

More blasts, until there was just one trite left, on Kane's leg. He looked at the head protrusion as it tried to gnaw on his skin.

Kane put the gun barrel right up to the thing's head and fired, sending pieces of it flying all over the room.

As soon as the attack ended, Kane sat down. He had a nasty new gash on his right leg, which, added to his other injuries, was—at the very least—going to make him hobble.

He dug out a small packet of gauze from his side pack. Two more stim injections were there too. He hesitated. That would leave only one, and that one he might need later.

He stuck the gauze on the wound, poured some antibiotic on the bandage, and then quickly taped it up, all the while looking around. The screams that filled this place continued, a mad keening that was the background noise of hell.

And when done, he quickly but painfully stood up. The right leg felt wobbly. *I'm falling part*, Kane thought.

He leveled his guns so both muzzles pointed dead ahead. After a while he lost any sense of how many things he had fought. He was down to one grenade, and he had reloaded three, maybe four times. His lower right pants leg dripped red, the bandage not doing much of anything.

Still he marched on.

There might come a time, he thought, when he

would recollect the horrors he saw. But for now, everything was meant to be seen and forgotten. He just followed the stench, the smells, the constant red light that seemed to creepily caress the skinlike "rock" of the ground, the walls, the ceiling of this subterranean madhouse.

And is there something above this . . . some world above these caves and tunnels? Or is this the whole world?

Every now and then he talked to himself, especially when he had killed something and had to walk over the oozing remains. Sometimes something simple, like *Good-bye.* Other times, almost as if angry, *Don't you ever, ever try to kill fucking me . . . Do you understand?* Then, shouting to the endless tunnels and caves: *"Do you understand?"*

He moved forward mostly on instinct, through the twisting nightmarish landscape. But the sounds, the screams, told him something was ahead.

Then he came to a tunnel opening, an immense one. The jumble of rocks and fire and creatures that filled it seemed to stretch forever.

He saw something that made him recoil, and he felt his eyes tear up. *Just maybe,* he thought, *I can't take any more.*

It was something akin to a corral. Jagged stone and rocks, shaped like rocky spikes, made a huge oval "fence." The fence surrounded humans, two dozen or so, all ages, all sexes, screaming, shaking.

And these other things walking around it. Guards? Was there any sense to anything he was seeing?

Then, as Kane watched, a headless creature with ragged bony protrusions covering its massive shape came up to the human corral. Kane watched as it speared one of the humans, and then it brought the human, still writhing, close to it and—somehow, some way—an opening appeared, and the human vanished *inside the thing*.

Kane's breathing became faster.

He looked to the right. More of the things stood there, perhaps waiting their turn to feed. And he looked at some of those waiting creatures he had fought before, the lumbering thing with tusks waddling around, and also the tall demonlike creatures with guns melded to their shoulders.

Then Kane saw it. On a table, standing there, beside what looked like an empty thronelike stone chair. Guarded, surrounded . . .

The Soul Cube.

Kane counted seconds in his head. Giving himself moments to think, to plan. But then those moments all vanished when he looked sharply left, then right.

On either side, a floating head, the teeth looking like nails, the eyes milky pools. Guards of a different kind, and they had spotted him. And now they screeched out a warning, and all within the chamber turned and saw *him*.

38

DR. AXELLE GRAULICH FELL TO HER KNEES. And for the first time she felt as if she knew what was happening now. After all, she could even hear the voices in her ears. The ancient sibilant sounds, the words that meant nothing.

But coupled with the swirling walls around her, the sounds told her that this place was indeed—now—ancient Mars. Dead for millions of years, maybe more, now somehow alive.

And those who used to inhabit the planet here, who vanished without a trace, were attempting to tell her what was happening.

"Please," she said, her hands rising up. "Tell me, speak to me."

The chorus of sounds were unintelligible. Now even the walls, which once sported symbols and marks, pulsed in time with the voices. She knelt there, knowing that they were trying to speak. The lost world of Mars was attempting to communicate.

She closed her eyes, thinking that if there was a way to communicate, a way she could understand, they would find it—and she should kneel in this place, which might not even exist, and wait, and listen.

UAC Headquarters

Ian Kelliher looked at the golden Labrador retriever circling the pod chamber, confused and scared, instinctively knowing that something was very wrong.

A voice in his ear: "Mr. Kelliher, we're ready, sir, on your command."

Kelliher hesitated. For the first time the laboratory here would attempt to replicate what happened on Mars, what Betruger had done. Was it the right thing to do? How could he be sure?

"Mr. Kelliher?"

"Okay. Doctor, whenever you are ready. Begin the transmission."

Two scientists went to a control station. Other UAC labs and offices around the world monitored the experiment also, getting all the data, ready to analyze every moment of what was about to happen. *Will it tell us everything?* Kelliher wondered. *Or nothing?*

One of the vid screens open before Kelliher

showed a close-up of the transporter screen. The distance from that to the target pod was the same critical distance as in Betruger's last, fatal tests. Theoretically, the same thing should happen.

Kelliher shifted in his seat. The screen flashed a new message: BEGINNING TELEPORTATION SEQUENCE. That message flashed for a bit; then it was replaced with:

TRANSMISSION IN 10 . . . 9 . . .

Another stray flicker of doubt filled Kelliher's brain. But at least he could tell himself that now it was too late. No turning back.

. . . 8 . . . 7 . . . 6 . . .

He thought of his father's warning. And the fact that Mars had gone off-line again. No comm connection in hours. Was there anything left up there?

. . . 5 . . . 4 . . . 3 . . .

Then a small PIP opened on the right screen.

An icon showing Mars. Below it the message: MARS CITY COMMUNICATION RESTORED.

Kelliher leaned forward. Mars back online. He'd hear what happened. And—

He looked at the dog inside the pod, now with both its paws raised up on the smooth, clear wall of the chamber, scratching, maybe moaning.

Mars online, just as this experiment was about to happen.

. . . 2 . . . 1 . . .

A voice in his ear from the UAC headquarters' satellite communications control. "Mr. Kelliher, we have contact, but we're getting strange power surges all—"

Kelliher started to speak. Not to his Comm Center, but to the scientist deep below the ground. But the countdown had run its course, and it was—of course—too late.

DELTA LAB

"You okay, Swann?" Campbell asked.

Swann nodded. "Just great. Fucking great."

"Hey, no need for foul language. See, it's nice and quiet here."

Swann shook his head. "I wish you had let me go with them, back to Reception."

"And leave me alone?" Campbell laughed. "You ain't much help, but I'll take what I can get. We will be here when Kane comes out."

"If he's even still alive; if he can even come back from there."

Campbell looked away. "We better hope he does. For everyone's sake. So we just sit here, and—" He stopped. There was a rumbling, almost like that of the tracks of a tank, or an armored vehicle. He looked at Swann, whose face brightened.

"Reinforcements!" Swann said.

Campbell listened. Yes, a lot like the sound of tank treads. But there were other sounds too, enough to make Campbell say: "I don't think so—"

And they both turned to the entrance to see what was heading into the lab.

•   •   •

Maria had one hand on Theo's shoulder, and they moved as one, his body joined to hers as they walked down the corridors.

"You okay?" she said.

"Yes."

"We have a ways to go, Theo. You understand?"

"Yes."

Maria took a breath. She never saw herself as the nurturing kind of woman. And she was pretty sure that kids weren't in her future. Now she tried to think what would reassure this boy, who had seen so much that was beyond belief, beyond understanding.

"You just stay nice and close, okay?" She gave his shoulder a slight squeeze. "We'll be all right."

But she didn't believe that at all.

The shrieking of the floating heads, yammering at Kane, became just one more thing to ignore. He quickly found out that a shotgun blast sent them flying away like balloons that had air escaping.

But the others below, the ones that now saw his arrival—different story there.

He realized too that he was in so much pain now that he didn't give a damn how much more pain he felt. *Just add it to my plate*, he thought.

Kane saw that the humans, the wretched creatures being plucked from the stone corral, looked up at him. Were they beyond hope? Did they think that they could survive, could be . . . saved? Does anyone ever really come back from hell?

He moved down the stone hill, strange gases shooting up, spraying him with a near-scalding steam.

Fuck it, he thought. *Just keep moving.*

He kept telling himself one thing: the chair was empty. Whatever, whoever, occupied that chair was *gone.* And that might be the best goddamned chance he had.

He didn't let that other thought sink in, the one that was really just too absurd to think about: that what he was doing might shape the fate of humanity.

For now, this was simply the thing that had to be done, the mission, the goddamned operation—that's all. And if there was one thing he knew about himself, once he signed on to a mission, he succeeded or he'd die trying.

Axelle. Kneeling in the great opening. Knowing now that this had once been a massive ceremonial hall, a place of science and religion for all those who lived here, back when Earth was still a toxic sea.

The sounds somehow clarifying, not into words but into images, nearly hallucinogenic in their clarity, their intensity. For the first time, she saw them, the beings who once called this home.

The sudden tears made her eyes go blurry. To see them, the first human to know that there was a time when others were here, and to know what they looked like . . .

Would she ever be able to tell people of their faces, the somewhat humanoid shape, but also so distinct, eyes and mouth never seen before? The way their limbs moved, as if each were saying—

No! she realized with a jolt. That movement *was* part of the way they communicated. And still—with only images and icons and feelings and flashes of the scene—they who were gone, who had vanished from here, quickly tried to tell Axelle their story.

She knelt there still, as if in prayer. Listening, and then wondering—

When they are done, whatever will I do with all they told me?

39

"NO," SWANN MOANED. "MY GOD—"

Campbell backed up, the BFG ready in one hand and a shotgun in the other. They each had a few grenades. He looked at what came into the room, flanked by a small squad of other creatures, each seven, eight feet tall, with guns *molded* to their shoulders.

"Campbell, we have to get—"

"Shut the fuck up, Swann."

The thing leading the squad roared to stop. *One for the books*, Campbell thought. The books of the perpetually insane and demented.

It was nothing less than a small tracked vehicle, a near-tank whose turret, as one moved up to it, resolved into the shape of a human. They were one thing, one being. And worse: Campbell knew who the being was. Or rather—used to be.

Sergeant Kelly—who had been the last bulwark stopping the hordes from Delta from getting through to the rest of the complex. Now, quite obviously, turned into one of them.

Not just one of them. Maybe there was some kind of twisted status in that Kelly was like this: part machine, part fucking tank, and part marine turned zombie. All these insane thoughts in an instant.

And in the next instant, Campbell started firing the BFG as rapidly as he could.

UAC Headquarters

Ian Kelliher knew that something bad was happening. He watched as his team tried to stop the transmission, but—whether due to fail-safe procedures or whether the system had somehow locked—the transmission continued.

At the same moment he could see the warnings about power surges throughout the UAC buildings, and then messages appeared warning about frequency spikes being sent out of the building.

The UAC network was probably more secure, more protected than even that used by the Pentagon. And yet—at this moment of transmission—signals filled with power surges, massive data packets, and who knew what else had simply . . . *left the building*.

Where the hell had they gone? Could they even find out? What was in them?

But soon his attention snapped back to the scene in the lab, the frantic scientists running around, and now the other chamber, glowing, the golden Labrador about to reappear. The test that caused all the protections of the fabled UAC network to fail . . . and allowed something to get out.

Kelliher felt sick. Instinctively he put a hand up to his mouth. He didn't want to see what would appear. But he knew he had to look.

And yes, the lab would get all the data from the "experiment." They might be able to analyze what had happened on Mars, what was still happening.

Something started to appear in the chamber.

Kelliher thought: *Have to contact the President. The fool. And Hakala. Need to speak to him. Need to plan, oh God, need to plan.*

The chamber filled with the familiar yellow-red glow.

The scientists, knowing that they had been too late to stop the transmission, now gathered near the chamber.

The scientists and Kelliher waited. Because in seconds, they'd all be able to see what had just been sent across the room, traveling the distance that they knew somehow changed the teleportation process.

It was a countdown of a different kind. One he wished would never end.

But then—on the screen—he could see . . .

Maria stopped. Two of the commando zombies, armed with standard US Space Marine issue, started raising their guns even as they walked toward them.

Maria did two things fast: she looked down at

Theo. If he bolted it could be a bad thing. But he stayed by her side, his eyes looking dead ahead at the lumbering creatures.

Then she quickly looked back to make sure that there weren't other things trying to get them in a trap. She couldn't see anything behind her. . . .

She did notice two small trites crawling in and out between the legs of the zombies. Could that mean there was one of the larger spiders around somewhere?

She waited just a second until their guns looked ready to fire, and then she pulled Theo to the right. The blasts from the zombies sprayed the center of the corridor with shells. Now Maria began firing, one-handed, drilling holes in the skulls of the things, sending sprays of whatever passed for blood and brain into the air.

"Close your eyes, Theo!" she shouted above the blasts.

The spider things started shrieking. A warning? Panic?

The trites were harder to hit as they started racing down the hallway, caroming off the sides crazily to avoid being hit. They behaved smarter than the zombies—that is, unless something out of sight was controlling them.

But when they crisscrossed, their tactical maneuver bringing them into the center of the hallway, she could target the center and have a good chance of hitting one. Which she did, and one trite exploded under the barrage.

The other kept up its crazy jumps back and forth.

But now Maria could concentrate on just that one. And with only meters left separating them, she finally started hitting the protrusion atop the spider-like carapace.

The trite slid to a stop, motionless at their feet.

She took a breath, and then looked down at Theo. "You can open your eyes now."

He looked up at her. "I never closed them."

She nodded, thinking that the boy had been changed by everything he'd seen. *And where will those changes lead?*

"Ready to go on?"

He nodded, and Maria, her hand still on his shoulder, led them down the hallway.

The mass of creatures, the mix of zombies and demons, the things shaped like a land walrus, slow and dull but deadly, the floating skull heads, shrieking and snapping—

They all acted to stop Kane, though maybe what was happening was unexpected. The idea that someone would actually get here.

Surprise, surprise.

Amid his blasts, the satisfying hits that ripped holes in the things and sent others flying backward, Kane shot out a section of the hellish corral, and the humans—gibbering, insane probably, but still human—started crawling out.

More confusion for these guardians of the Soul Cube.

The confusion was good, helping Kane reach the cube. He scrambled up the last few feet, dodging blasts from the demons with their small cannons molded to their upper torsos.

Maybe it was his lack of fear, the fact that nothing he saw could scare him. Or perhaps it was his sense from so many battles on Earth that surprise can indeed be *everything*. Maybe it was the lucky break of freeing the crazed beings, the human food, the living morsels they fed upon, that probably somehow powered them.

Or perhaps it was all three of those things.

But Kane now reached the stone chair, molded to fit a massive creature that wasn't there—and beside it, the Soul Cube.

He grabbed it. And in that moment he felt its power. The responsibility. The cries. The sacrifice of millions. All funneled into this item that stopped the invasion from hell last time.

Kane spun around quickly. Some of the freed humans looked at him for help. They could be a liability. But if being human meant anything, it was the ability to care for others, to give a damn for your fellow creatures.

The defenders of this cavern swirled around him in confusion, easy targets. Kane tried to say the words to the freed humans: *Follow me.*

But his mouth was too dry, with only the dusty taste of his own salt, blood spatters, and who knew what else.

When he started moving back to the opening, it was more than clear to those few humans left what they should do.

For Axelle, the terrible story was clear. The proud and wonderful Martian race sacrificing itself, channeling all its power, what we would call their "souls," into this device that was part extraordinary weapon and part fantastic mystical device. They all had to do it so that it could be wielded by one of them, one lone hero. Each and every one, feeding the weapon.

Abandoning their planetary existence to stop this. To seal the evil away with this ward of psychic power that was a million years—if not more—beyond our comprehension.

A sacrifice for the ages.

And the images and sounds that filled her head told her that, with the cube removed, gone and taken back to the other universe, there was no hope.

Ahead, she could see the reflected glow. The opening, the massive open wound that would lead to the place of monsters and madness.

And then Axelle had one hopeful thought: *I have survived until now, in this nether region between Mars and some death universe. It has to have been for a purpose. . . .*

Such a human delusion, a voice inside her head suggested.

But she pushed that voice away and clung to the thought, delusion or not.

40

WHAT WAS ONCE A GOLDEN LABRADOR retriever was now yet another new creature that had never been seen before. The lower jaw protruded as if it had—Pinocchio-like—grown, curving up like the maw of a prehistoric creature.

And there, on the dog's back, another opening, a two-foot-long gash lined with teeth, opening and shutting, each shutting signaled by a terrible snap.

The dog's paws now three-toed claws, each ending in perfectly curved hooks.

The dog reared up and began to scratch at the chamber wall. All the scientists recoiled. The chamber wall should be able to resist nearly anything. But for a second it looked as if this thing might smash through the explosive-resistant polymer material. And wouldn't that be fun?

"Kill it," Ian Kelliher ordered. "Kill the damn thing now."

They had a number of different methods to do that, but the lead scientist in the lab down below went for the most direct method. He threw a switch, and the chamber became filled with electric spikes dancing around, spearing and skewering the monstrosity until it finally stopped its incessant clawing at the chamber wall. And lay down, dead.

Nobody said or did anything for a moment.

Then Dr. Adoni said: "Sir, we got all the data. We can begin—"

Kelliher shut off the audio.

They got all the data. But in that moment, the very moment of the transmission, something was sent out of the lab . . . and around the world. To where, to how many places, and God, what was it that was sent?

Kelliher sat in the room, the screens now all quiet. And planned what he had to do next.

The radio was on, and Campbell could hear the chatter in his ear.

But above that he heard the clanking of the treads that were now the tanklike lower part of Sergeant Kelly's body.

He started firing, sending a steady spray of the massive shells at the rolling monstrosity.

And the thing could still speak as Kelly screamed with each blast that hit it, yelling above the blasting gun, "Master Sergeant Thomas Kelly . . . reporting for duty!"

"Jeezus," Swann said.

"Fire your damn gun," Campbell ordered.

Campbell leveled the BFG right at Sergeant Kelly's head when he was blindsided by a shell that hit his left shoulder, the blast sending him flying to the ground.

Something to the side, he thought. *I wasn't watching. Must have come at me when I wasn't looking. . . .*

Now he could see what it was: one of the tall demons, guns on its shoulders. It could have kept firing, but it stood there, waiting.

The treads kept clacking away, closer. The voice, again, "Master Sergeant Thomas Kelly . . . reporting for duty!"

Campbell noticed that Swann was beside him, dead. *Didn't even hear that blast,* Campbell thought. He tried to raise the BFG, but now it was too heavy.

And he knew why the demon just loomed over him, waiting. He was Kelly's to kill.

Campbell tried once again to move the gun, and then he tried to dig out his handgun. He felt his fingers touch the gun handle, and then the tanklike tracks stopped. And then the blasts from Kelly made everything vanish.

Maria walked with the boy out to Reception, and everyone standing there turned and looked at her.

For a minute she wondered if they might think that she was one of them. Her face was spattered with blood, and Theo's clothes were in tatters, his eyes hollow. She stood there and waited. Would they just stare at her, stand there—and goddamn it, that's all?

But a soldier walked over to her. He looked from Maria to the boy, then back to her eyes. *What stories do my eyes tell?* she thought. *Are the nightmares so easily read in my eyes?*

Then the soldier turned and bellowed at the waiting crowd. "Medical, get the hell over here." He turned back to Maria and Theo, speaking to both of them. "It's going to be okay. You're safe now. It's all going to be all right."

Words of reassurance.

And Maria didn't have the energy left to tell him how hollow those words sounded.

Kane climbed back to the opening, taking care to retrace his steps. And with every creature he killed he saw how the artifact he carried, the Soul Cube, glowed, as if the death of these things powered it.

And when one of the guardian creatures tried to attack Kane, he could fire the cube at it, watching the way a starlike burst sliced into the creature. The guardian screamed out at the contact, and reared back as the ancient weapon cut into it.

The humans Kane had freed scrambled to keep up with him. But he couldn't pause to help them. They had to get out on their own, because what he had to do was more important.

He tried not to wonder if Delta would still be guarded when he came out. Could he go from Delta, and leave Mars City, to take the Soul Cube back to where it belonged? Did he have enough time, enough energy, left to do that?

He turned again to fire at creatures scrambling after him. As each one fell, and the cube began to glow stronger, they seemed to hold back. If something was going to stop him, it wouldn't be them.

The cave—alive with voices—took on a deeper glow as a swirling vortex appeared before Axelle and like an iris began to open.

The voices in Axelle's mind screamed out with each widening of the bloodred iris.

There's nothing I can do, Axelle wanted to say. *I can only watch this.* And she knew what it was. She knew that before her eyes, the ancient opening to hell was being reborn.

What would come through that opening?

Kelliher repeated the name . . . "Campbell?"

There was no answer from Mars City, though the radio communications were up and running. General Hayden tried again to speak to Kelliher, and again Kelliher let the general's voice hang in the air unanswered.

Then: "Karla, do you have the President's office?"

"Yes, sir. Just waiting on you, then they will patch you through directly to the President."

"Good. Let's do it."

Kelliher wondered how the President would react

when he heard what Kelliher would ask for, what he wanted to happen to his dream for the UAC—his dream really for the future of humanity—*Mars City*.

He waited, and then an image of the President appeared, already looking as though he knew something really bad was ahead.

"Mr. President . . ." Kelliher began.

41

KANE REACHED THE OPENING, THE PORTAL that led back to Delta. He could see that it now seemed smaller, as though with time it were losing energy. Only temporary—soon to be replaced with something more permanent. If he let that happen.

He heard people yelling behind him—the survivors. But he couldn't stop and wait—so he just stepped in—

—and through to the other side.

To where Campbell should have been standing with the massive gun. Instead Kane, stepping out of the open chamber, saw Swann, half his body blown away, sprawled near the open chamber door.

And Campbell? Kane scanned the room and thought: *Need that gun, buddy. Could* really *use that gun where I'm going.*

He spotted another body halfway across the lab, close to the wall. Campbell, looking like someone went to town with him, drilling holes everywhere.

Then a noise filled the room, an incessant clacking echoing in the empty lab.

Kane spun around to see . . .

What was once Sergeant Kelly, now some kind of horrific tank creature. Bad enough, but worse was that Kelly held the BFG in his one hand that still looked normal.

"Private, atten-*tion*!" The words garbled, guttural. Then Kelly screamed them again. *"Private!"*

Now the BFG, wavering in the hand of the Kelly creature, started chewing holes in the metal floor.

Two skeletal demons appeared, one armored only with its claws, the other with cannonlike guns part of its body. They came at Kane from the other end, and he realized that he had walked into a classic pincer movement. But none of the creatures seemed to have noticed what Kane held in his hand.

As Kane rolled right, sliding to the ground to avoid the burst from each end of the pincer, he heard a voice in his mind as the cube glowed: *Use us!*

He aimed the cube at one of the demons and pressed the artifact where it glowed. And suddenly a star-shaped burst of light flew out of the Soul Cube, directly for the center of the demon, annihilating it.

In just one shot, Kane thought. The other demon hesitated, and Kane turned back to Kelly, now maneuvering its armored body at Kane, ready to bear down.

The Soul Cube glowed again, and Kane pressed the spot.

And now, fed by the force of the creatures he had killed—and whatever the great Martian race did to create this weapon—he watched another brilliant star rocket out of the Soul Cube and smash into Kelly's upper torso. This time the burst punched a hole in the flesh, and Kane could see right through the plate-sized cavity.

Kelly's eyes blinked, and then his tank lower torso ground to a halt. His left hand dropped the BFG.

Kane fired one last blast from the Soul Cube, and Kelly's upper torso was blown off the tank.

Kane ran up and grabbed the gun, a massive weight, even with the heavy shoulder strap bearing some of the load. And with the gun held in his right hand and the Soul Cube in his left, Kane left Delta Lab, the portal already closing behind him, and hurried to the nearby exterior access, to leave Mars City . . . and to face whatever waited for him at Site 3.

THE BATTLE CRUISER
NEAR MARS

Captain Hakala sat in his chair as the signals from both Mars City and Earth began filtering into the ship's comm system.

The messages that had built up during the silence started arriving at a dizzying rate. He had a number of his analysts on the data, looking at what was happening on the Red Planet, floating before him, as well as messages from Earth.

But a live contact suddenly cut through the flow.

His communications officer came up to him. "Mr. Kelliher, Captain. On a secure line."

Hakala wondered if there would be a delay or any distortion. Sometimes when the comm system rebooted, it took a while before instantaneous conversations could take place.

"Mr. Kelliher."

"Captain, status report on your battle cruiser?"

"Sir, we are prepared to land for the planetary evac on your—"

"No, Captain. The battle-ready state?"

"All weapons systems active and fully engaged. I have landing parties all equipped. We're ready for whatever we find down there."

"Missile warheads, Captain?"

Hakala stopped. Missiles? What was Kelliher talking about?

"Mr. Kelliher, I haven't readied the missile teams, or plotted any target trajectory, sir. I'm afraid I'm a little confused. What exactly—"

"Captain, you will be getting a confirming order from the President of the United States, coauthorized by Defense Secretary Simmons. You are to plot and target the planet for an immediate attack."

"Attack? Sir? Those are our people down there. Civilians, scientists, other marines. You can't—"

"Perhaps I'm not making myself perfectly clear. You will have orders to plan the destruction of Mars City, the obliteration of everything on that planet.

You will carry out those orders without question, and on my immediate order—or your superiors will have you replaced. Am I clear now?"

Hakala looked at the screen showing Kelliher, and he wondered, *What the hell happened on Mars?* He had thought the Armada had come to reinforce the brigades there, perhaps transport civilians off the planet. Now they were to destroy it?

Was what had happened exclusively on Mars, or did something also happen on Earth?

"Yes, sir. I understand. I will order all preparations to be made, bringing the missile systems into readiness and ready for your command."

"Good. You should be receiving your confirming orders in minutes. And in approximately sixty minutes, I will give the command."

Hakala took a breath. Sixty minutes, and every living thing on the planet below would be destroyed.

"I will stand by, sir."

Kelliher's screen flashed off, and Hakala sat there for a moment, numb.

Kane placed the EVA helmet on and twisted it tight. He checked that the HUD inside showed the two canisters of air, and that the outside reading systems worked fine.

He stood inside the airlock, ready to make his way to Site 3. There were other ways to the excavation area, he imagined, but he thought, *I'm new here. So this way will have to do.*

And there was one thing to do before leaving.

"Maria Moraetes," he said. A bit of squelch in the earpiece. Then he was connected. "Maria, you okay?"

"Kane, where are you? We're fine. What happened?"

"Much to explain, Maria. But not now. You and Theo got back to Reception okay?"

"Yes. Kane, your voice sounds muffled, almost—"

"Got a helmet on. Have to step outside for a while."

"Outside? Out on the surface?"

"Listen, Maria, I can't talk any more. We don't have the time. But if I'm successful—and I will find a way to let you know—then it will be safe for the Armada to come. Tell Hayden. It will be okay. But only if I succeed." A breath. "You understand what I mean?"

Would Maria know the implications of Kane not returning, and what it meant to Mars City? Absolutely, he thought. "Maria, I'll come back if I can."

A hesitation at her end. "You better."

"So—" Now a long pause from him. "Bye for now."

"B—" she started.

But he had already turned the radio off. He wanted no signals being picked up as he made his way to the excavation site. He engaged the airlock.

42

KANE WALKED PAST THE DEAD SCIENTISTS, their bodies twisted in their EVA suits. *Compared to many, they're actually the lucky ones,* he thought.

He gave the BFG's shoulder strap a small heft, trying to work it up closer to his neck. And in the other hand, the Soul Cube, its glow a bit reduced now. Clearly, the more creatures that were taken out, the stronger it became.

And the voices? Though they were now quiet, Kane could feel them with him. He thought, *Someone, someday, will write the history of the great Martian civilization and its amazing sacrifice. That is, if anyone here survives.*

Deep into the cave now, Kane saw the markings that filled the excavation site's walls, all incomprehensible, icons with no meaning, swirls and squiggles darting in every direction.

He saw how, the deeper he went, the brighter they became. Though his march deep into the cave seemed to have no impact on the Soul Cube, perhaps the cave itself was responding?

He looked down at the cube, then the BFG, wondering: Would they be enough? The time to find that out drew close.

At the site of the last excavation point, the cave gave way to an opening that led sharply down, and then twisted away even deeper into Mars.

Not very inviting, Kane thought. Once he stepped into it, he would more than likely slide down until he reached whatever was at the end of the twisting tunnel.

But now the cube seemed to flash brighter, as if sensing that it was close to where it belonged. The artifact, dubbed U1 when found, might be the only thing that saved Mars. Kane leaned over the edge, wondering if he could carefully navigate his way down. His bones and muscles hurt in so many places, it almost didn't matter what body part he favored.

There was no easy way down. He took a step, almost like a diver stepping into the abyss of the deep ocean, and in the next moment, weapons clasped tight, he was tumbling head over heels, rolling into the unknown.

Kane came to a stop and scurried to his feet, imagining that a deadly welcoming committee might be there. But this part of the tunnel was still empty. He could see that it led to a great glowing area ahead, as if lit by a thousand flickering candles.

With his first step, he heard the voices again, the words alien, the sounds unknown to the human ear, and yet . . . they conveyed fear, and hope . . . and a mix of emotions that nearly clouded Kane's head.

He walked, nearly limping, into the great room ahead, the sound of the voices swelling.

He wanted to speak back to them, to say, *I will try. Because, after all, that's all I can do.*

He repeated that mantra in his mind a few more times. *I will try.*

Then something from his past emerged, a different mantra from so many battles in the past, some bit of combat propaganda drilled into new recruits from day one of their admission into the corps.

Failure isn't an option. Damn right, Kane thought. Damn right.

Axelle opened her eyes. She looked down at the cave floor, now so many feet below.

What happened? she thought. Her body was wrapped in a tight webbing that held her arms and legs in close. But her head was free, and she could look around the room.

And she saw it—the portal, swirling, growing— and only then did she wonder: *Why am I here? Why am I still alive?*

Kane stopped in the room. Only seconds to take it all in, this massive room with what looked like a map of glittering stars from unknown constellations high above him.

And the opening, the portal, pulsing, growing with

every tornadolike swirl. The real path to hell, the roadway to doom, now being made permanent. No creatures yet, he thought. Maybe there was still time.

But then he looked up and to his right—and saw her.

A woman floating, levitating in the room as if hung by a thousand invisible lines. Her body was wrapped tight, nearly cocoonlike. But she could look down at Kane, could see him, her eyes looking down so amazingly peaceful from her floating prison.

She was breathing. There was air here.

He took off his helmet. "I'll help you!" he shouted up to her, taking a fateful step in that direction.

She quickly shook her head and started shouting at him.

"No. You have to stop *that*. The way they did—one armed with all the souls of Mars. But—but—it's here!"

The words registered as Kane tensed. *It's. Here.*

A pair of winged demons, small, with infantile heads, fluttered up to the woman. Their claw hands dug at the webbing, exposing her body, but she still floated. Then their infant heads split open, exposing massive teeth.

Kane raised the BFG and started blasting, but as he caught the first two, another pair flew close, then two more, blocking her. The woman screamed, and Kane raised the Soul Cube, thinking it was already too late to save her.

It's. Here.

In that moment he recognized this for what it was. A trap.

He spun around, and there, behind him, so close, towering over him, undaunted, a full thirty feet tall—

A demon like none Kane had seen. One arm ended in a cannon, and while its protective carapace shifted as it started to aim and fire, the cannon blasts blew into the ground near Kane.

He barely dodged the first blast, and he kept rolling on the ground, awkwardly rolling over the BFG, but knowing that to stop moving would make him an easy target.

The mammoth demon—the thing that must have occupied the throne in hell—took a leap in Kane's direction, and when it landed, the ground shook.

Kane saw other things coming out of the vortex. The party was beginning, and he was on the ground, nearly atop his gun, useless.

The woman's screams had ended. But her word of warning, that millisecond of warning, had saved Kane's life. Now what would he do with that chance?

The Soul Cube spoke again in a single voice, the meaning clear even if there were no actual words: *Use us . . . use us!*

Kane stood up for his final battle.

The demon waved one six-foot arm in the air, directing its new arrivals, all taking positions in this room, and soon to fill the planet, and eventually this very universe.

Use us.

A few eager imps appeared and started circling movements around Kane, toying with him. But he spun around with them as if in an ancient dance, finally holding the BFG up, the trigger held as the gun fired, kicking some imps back against the wall and punching plate-sized holes in others.

Others from the mammoth demon's troops hesitated, seeing their brothers cut down. Everything alive—no matter with what kind of life—wants to stay alive, Kane thought. Even things from hell.

But the giant demon used that feint to move close, its carapace again shifting, rearranging its layers of plate armor. The cannon arm locked into a position, clear and straight, perfect for aiming.

Kane ripped off his last grenade and tossed it, hoping to send it right down the wide bore of the demon's gun. But he missed, and instead the grenade detonated at the demon's feet. But the blast made the cannon arm fly up, screwing up its perfect aim.

Other than that, the grenade hadn't at all penetrated the armorlike plates on the thing's body.

Can it talk? Kane wondered. *Communicate? Or does it have the empty single-mindedness of a warrior ant, ripping an opponent apart for food?*

Now, in the only time left—these few seconds before the creatures in the room would be emboldened to swarm and kill Kane and more cannon shots came—Kane raised the Martian Soul Cube.

The life force of the entire planet was embedded

inside it, a ward against evil that transcended time and space.

Kane held the artifact up. He aimed at the giant demon king—if that's what it was—and began firing.

The first starlike blast from the cube caromed off the armor, and Kane thought that even this great weapon was useless against the demon.

A half dozen trites—the front lines of their final attack—had scurried to Kane's legs, looking to grab on and close their viselike legs on him.

He couldn't be distracted. He thought of what he told Maria: *If I come back, it will be safe. If not . . .*

Then, as if trying to get his completely exhausted mind to focus, the unspoken words again, so clear: *Use . . . us!*

He fired the Soul Cube again, and this time he saw a star blast create an opening in the layers of armor plating. Like any machine or vehicle, this monster had its weak point. The blast alarmed it and it looked down, and Kane saw liquid rocket out.

"Yeah, hurts like a bitch," Kane said. And hearing his own voice made him feel somehow stronger. "Have another."

Another blast from the cube rocketed out, and this one too found a weak spot. The demon fired a cannon blast, but even with the trites holding on, Kane stepped away.

He took a moment and aimed the BFG at the trites, taking care not to blow off any parts of his own body. One had crawled up to Kane's midsection, and Kane let the BFG dangle from his shoulder, grabbed his handgun, placed the muzzle right at the head of the thing, and fired.

He quickly returned his attention to the giant demon. It waved its arms again, signaling those who had arrived. But the other creatures, the foot soldiers of demons and imps and trites, moved slowly.

"Just you and goddamn me," Kane said.

The Soul Cube glowed at its brightest, and Kane fired it again. Another shot found its mark, this time near the knees of the thing, more metal and machine than demon's skin. But still an opening was found.

The creature fell to one knee, and now Kane could see the thing's head tilt. He wondered: *Is this the ruler, or just a grunt, some lieutenant from hell about to pay the price for an invasion gone wrong?*

"Say good-bye. . . ."

Another star blast from the cube raced to the thing's head, to the open maw gasping from the wounds it had received.

And that head exploded, sending chunks of the thing, along with the metal parts of its body, flying into the air.

The room was still full of creatures. But now, this part . . . this part would be easy.

He turned and started firing, and kept firing, screaming with each kill, relentless in this ancient room.

43

WHEN THIS GREAT CEREMONIAL ROOM OF THE Martian civilization was filled with the dead bodies of the invaders, Kane walked up to the portal, still twisting, swirling.

He wasn't sure what to do, and the woman who had saved him from the demon's attack was gone. The cube itself glowed with massive power, but told him no secrets.

He fired at the portal, and a bright flash disappeared into it. Kane watched it shrink, like a slug recoiling from salt. Okay, that seemed to work.

Then another, and another, until, like a spiderweb swept away in some forgotten corner, the portal was gone. The room was quiet.

And the Soul Cube? Quite clearly that should stay right here, Kane thought. In this warren of caves, to make sure that hell never tried to come to Mars again.

He took one last look at the room. Probably a good idea to recommend that this cave be sealed. Though he had to wonder: What were the chances of that?

His fatigue, his total exhaustion, along with dozens

of wounds small and large, made the idea of getting back to Mars City seem impossible. But then he told himself: *I seem to be doing pretty well at the impossible today.*

Walking slowly, taking care not to bend in places where it would cause even more excruciating pain, he headed back.

The climb up to the surface almost stopped Kane. Then he remembered that his supply pack came with a utility knife. Not much of a knife, but enough to dig into the soft wall and ground to help pull himself up. And when he saw Mars City, he actually started to hurry.

He opened his radio link. "Okay, Maria. You can organize mop-up in there. No more creatures will be coming. I'm guessing some of them there . . . may have disappeared."

No answer. Complete silence.

"Maria? Maria, you getting this?"

He switched to another frequency. "Is anyone picking this up? Come in? What the hell—"

What lay ahead? he wondered. What had happened while he was gone?

He shut the airlock door and waited while the system removed the thin gas of the Martian surface and replaced it with air. He took off the helmet. When the display screen flashed CLEAR FOR REENTRY, Kane opened the door to Mars City.

He would have a long way to go, but at least he was inside.

He tried his radio again: "Is anyone here? Anyone picking this up?"

He walked with the gun barrel pointed down; he'd remember that, the gun down, his guard down. More concerned about the others than himself. "Is there no one on the damn radio?"

He moved down the corridor and came to a T. He turned left, which would lead him past the Marine Command Center and eventually to Mars City Reception.

"Kane! Kane, you there?"

It was Hayden. "General, yes, I've just—"

"Yes, we know, Kane. Most of the creatures are gone. Whatever you did worked. Only the infected humans remain. And only a few of them. It's over. We alerted the Armada. Your radio wasn't picking us up for some reason."

Good, Kane thought. *It's over.* And there was no need for a Plan B. And he could well imagine what that was.

"Moraetes, sir. Is she—?"

"What, don't you—"

The Armada was coming. All was good. And sometimes, that's when bad things can happen.

Kane heard the repetitive shots of a chain gun and saw his lower right leg get blown off. He screamed as blood gushed from the massive wound below his knee.

Through the pain, he saw the crazed lone zombie

with its gun, moving closer, ready for another shot. Which was when the zombie was cut down, arms flailing as an incessant rain of shells was fired into it.

Kane closed his eyes. *Sleep*, he thought.

"Kane, Kane!"

He opened his eyes. A stim needle was sticking out of his arm.

He shifted his gaze, and saw Maria. He opened his mouth and tried to speak, but nothing came out.

"I bandaged the wound. You lost a lot of blood. Going to get you to Reception. They have a med team . . . going to meet us."

Then he remembered. He tried to form the words. "My . . . leg."

Maria's eyes, he could see, were wet. She shook her head.

"Nothing left," said Kane. "I'm all shot up. I'm sorry, so—"

She looked around. "I gotta get you out of here. Not safe. Even with most of the things gone."

He nodded. She started to pull him up, all that deadweight. "No," he croaked, "too . . . heavy."

"Yeah. I know. Heavy." She grunted, working her right shoulder under his left arm. When she had him, and could barely carry him down the hallway, she said, "You owe me, Kane. You goddamn owe me. . . ."

And with those last words, he closed his eyes.

EPILOGUE

44

ANDY KIM STOOD CLOSE TO MARIA AS THEY watched the line of wounded being wheeled into the transport shuttle that would bring these marines and civilians back to Earth.

"Not a lot of them," he said.

She turned to Andy, lost in her own thoughts. "What? What do you mean?"

"Not a lot of wounded. People either got killed or got turned into zombies."

She nodded.

"That Kane guy—he's lucky."

Lucky, she thought? To have his leg blown off? And when he was so close to getting back, to being safe? Of course they can do amazing things with the intelligent prosthetics. Still, for Kane, it would be hard.

She had asked if she could ship back to Earth, trying

not to let General Hayden know that she might have some feelings for the man who had saved Mars City.

But Hayden's answer was sharp and to the point. *No*. There was way too much to do up here. As soon as Kane closed the portal at Site 3, the creatures simply vanished except for those once-humans who stumbled around still looking for something to attack.

By now, the surviving space marines were experienced with taking those things down.

But with so much of Mars City a wreck, and with so many miles of corridors to clear, it would be days before they would know they had cleared everywhere. Then there would be the reports, and— Hayden reminded Maria—she, at this point, knew more than almost anyone else here.

She would stay. End of discussion. Oh, there was one perk. She'd be given a promotion. Hayden wasn't sure exactly what yet, but she should be glad of that.

So, from a distance, she watched them wheel the sleeping Kane into the underbelly of the transport.

"I mean," Kim said, "that guy there just saved us. He's like some whacked-out Jesus."

Jesus with a shotgun, Maria thought. "Yeah, he did save us. And everyone here better goddamn remember that."

"Hey, easy, Moraetes. I like the guy."

She smiled. "Okay. Sorry. And you, Andy, you okay?"

"Well, I still hurt when I breathe or move. Other than that, I'm just fine."

Another smile. It felt good to smile. With all the death, the memorial services to come, the investigations sure to come, best to grab every small smile you can.

After the wounded, others filed into the shuttle—the lucky ones, eager to get off Mars and away from Mars City as soon as possible.

She saw one of the nurses from the infirmary walking with Theo. She had to wonder what all this would do to the boy. Forget the nightmares, the waking up, remembering everything that he had really seen . . . what would it do to him when he grew up? What would happen when he was home, alone?

She remembered how close he had clung as she brought him back. Clinging tightly to her but nonetheless walking so steadily. Maria had promised she would check up on him back on Earth. *Life goes on. Or at least, we hope so.*

"Hey, what about the scientist who ran Delta, that Betruger guy? They find him?"

"Nope. Not yet." Maria shrugged. "Maybe he's dead. Maybe he got sucked into the place where those things came from."

She still found it hard to use the word that everyone else had already started using: "hell."

"Or maybe he's still here somewhere," Andy said. "Maybe we'll find him. I'd like a piece of that maniac."

Wouldn't we all, Maria thought. She turned to Kim. "Come on, Andy. Let's get back to work."

Kim laughed as he turned away from the transport and started following her. "Work? Work? Is that what you call what we do up here? That's funny. . . ."

And they walked back to the marine barracks, where the mourning had only begun.

TOMMY KELLIHER'S ESTATE
NEWPORT BEACH

Ian Kelliher stood outside the door to his father's office, which also served as a hospital dayroom armed with all the medical equipment that might be needed to keep his father alive.

He didn't have to come here so quickly but he knew that his father had his own internal UAC spies even though he was fully retired from the company and the board.

So he'd have to tell him everything. About the losses on Mars and the death totals that rose and rose. About the doorway that opened to another world, another universe. About how the Martian civilization from millions of years ago sacrificed itself to stop them. And how what they did had to be done again. About how he had come so close to giving an order that would have left Mars a nuclear wasteland for generations.

About how the lone ex-lieutenant—the disgraced John Kane—nearly single-handedly saved us all.

And then finally . . .

About the desperate experiments done right at the Palo Alto headquarters . . . and how something, somehow, had gone wrong. And how no one knew what had happened—or what it meant—yet.

The twin doors to Tommy Kelliher's office opened. A nurse in bright starched whites looked at Ian and said, "Mr. Kelliher can see you now."

Ian walked in to tell his father everything.

BALLARD STATION
THE MID-ATLANTIC RIDGE

Everyone had gone without sleep for over a day now, David knew. And somewhere in the middle of their work, they got the message that it was over on Mars.

Julie had turned to him and asked, "Guess they'll want all these scientists back now, hm?"

David shook his head. "I don't know. Maybe. Maybe not."

Dr. Watanabe's team from Tokyo had quickly started working on the symbiotic process at the micro level. And Elaina Krasanov worked alongside him, both lost in the work.

The scientific firepower gathered around that one lab table was nothing short of incredible.

That they were about to make a breakthrough so fast, even more so.

"We think we have something," Krasanov said to

David. "We're tired, and we've looked at it a number of times, but Watanabe and his team agree, it's *something*."

David had also gone without sleep, fueling his monitoring of all the teams with as much caffeine as possible. "Let me get Dr. Chao."

"Certainly."

David grabbed Julie and they hurried over to the table where Krasanov had been designated spokesperson.

"The interesting thing, a confusing thing, was how the toxic bacteria essentially bonds with the normal organics of the tube worm—or any of the similar creatures of the hydrothermal vents. We watched, we analyzed, but nothing."

Watanabe raised a finger.

"Yes, then Dr. Watanabe said something that redirected the whole team: What if it isn't 'bonding'?"

"Hm?" David said.

"Not a symbiotic relationship at all, but more a merger where they become one. And if they are *one*, then there aren't really two systems going on, but one new system—one that we hadn't seen before."

David looked at Julie. In all their years of working with the vent samples, it was an idea that hadn't occurred to them. Maybe because it seemed impossible.

"But for that to happen—"

And Watanabe, certainly the oldest scientist at

the station, took a step closer. "Right, impossible." His English was heavily accented, but understandable. "The—" He said something in Japanese to one of his team, who responded with the English word. "Yes, David, the 'breakthrough' ideas often are impossible."

David had so many questions. "But if the host and parasite become one system, then one of them has their biology taken over, or maybe both?"

Watanabe nodded. His eyes were deep, his face covered with wrinkles. "Yes. Or perhaps something else happens."

Krasanov continued: "Whatever it is, David, once we looked at it as one unified system, with the new hybrid creature one thing, then everything we've seen—everything you've seen—made sense. It all fell into place."

Julie spoke up: "And now . . . what are the implications?"

Krasanov smiled at her, a look that said none of them had really thought a lot about the implications yet. But: "Oh yes. Those." A smile. "We can't even imagine what they are—not yet."

David nodded. "Good work. All of you. I will let UAC know. But maybe we should all grab some sleep now?"

Watanabe turned away.

"There will be time for sleep . . . later."

David and Julie watched as the team turned away . . . and returned to work.

ABOARD THE MARTIAN TRANSPORT

Kane's eyes fluttered open. He had remembered them giving him blood, and meds through an IV. And enough painkillers that while he felt a nagging pain from his right leg, it didn't feel that bad at all. . . .

Just a scratch.

But he knew that if the painkillers ever really wore off, his screams would fill this room.

With difficulty he now turned to look at the room he was in. And he immediately saw that he was in the infirmary of a big ship. Not the battle cruiser itself, but a larger transport than they normally sent. He also could see the beds around him.

Not that many, he thought. *Not many survivors. Is this it?* he wondered. *Or are others on Mars being treated there?*

But he had seen the carnage, the bodies. *This* was it. The lucky few who had survived.

A nurse at a far end of the room moved from bed to bed, the lighting subtle, the room hushed. So many questions he wanted answered. And they would have so many questions for him.

But for now, as Mars receded behind him, John Kane felt the pain start to return. He hit the button that fed the drips of medicine into a vein.

In seconds, he felt the inexorable pull of sleep, blessed sleep.

ABOUT THE AUTHOR

MATTHEW COSTELLO'S work includes innovative and critically acclaimed novels, games, and television shows. His novel *Beneath Still Waters* was filmed by Lionsgate in 2007, and his latest original novel is *Nowhere*. He's written for PBS, The Disney Channel, The Sci-Fi Channel, and the BBC, among others. He's scripted dozens of bestselling and award-winning games, including *The 7th Guest, Doom 3*, and *Pirates of the Carribbean: At World's End*. You can learn more at www.mattcostello.com.